I0619647

Tales from the Canyons of the Damned Omnibus 12

PRESENTED BY USA TODAY BESTSELLING AUTHOR
DANIEL ARTHUR SMITH

This book is a work of fiction and any resemblance to persons, living or dead, is purely coincidental. Tales from the Canyons of the Damned All rights reserved Holt Smith ltd Collection Copyright © 2022 by Daniel Arthur Smith

The Patron Saint by Steven Van Patten. Copyright © 2019. Steven Van Patten. Used by permission of the author.

EV 2000 by Amy Grech. Copyright © 2020. Amy Grech. Used by permission of the author.

The Fear of a Z'n – A story of Altiva by Teel James Glenn. Copyright © 2018. Teel James Glenn. Used by permission of the author.

Boys in the Basement by Jessica West. Copyright © 2020 Jessica West. Used by permission of the author.

The Invader by Daniel Arthur Smith. Copyright © 2020 Daniel Arthur Smith. Used by permission of the author.

Voodoo Queen by Steve Oden. Copyright © 2021. Steve Oden. Used by permission of the author.

Talk Box by Ernie Howard. Copyright © 2021. Ernie Howard. Used by permission of the author.

Absolute Dark by Paul B. Kohler. Copyright © 2021. Paul B. Kohler. Used by permission of the author.

The End… Again by Jessica West. Copyright © 2021 Jessica West. Used by permission of the author.

The Lost Tapes – Arrow Lake and True Millennial by Daniel Arthur Smith. Copyright © 2021 Daniel Arthur Smith. Used by permission of the author.

Bloody Bridge by Steve Oden. Copyright © 2021. Steve Oden. Used by permission of the author.

Gibberlings by Charles Barouch. Copyright © 2021. Charles Barouch. Used by permission of the author.

Under Denver by Hunter C. Eden. Copyright © 2021. Hunter C. Eden. Used by permission of the author.

Cover Design By Daniel Arthur Smith Special thanks to Jessica West

 ISBN-13: 978-1-946777-91-1

For Susan, Tristan, & Oliver, as all things are.

38

Tales from the Canyons of the Damned

FEATURING

AMY GRECH

JESSICA WEST

STEVEN VAN PATTEN

TEEL JAMES GLENN

PRESENTED BY USA TODAY BESTSELLING AUTHOR

DANIEL ARTHUR SMITH

The Patron Saint

Steven Van Patten

THEY SAT ACROSS FROM one another on opposite ends of the center island counter. Five feet of glass mosaic tile stood between them. They sat in silence, eyes downcast, each of them absorbed in their own flavor of shame. An ex-husband who had failed to protect his daughter. An ex-wife who had fallen for a smooth-talking opportunist.

"I'm sorry," Cathy said.

"You're sorry?" Keith mocked. "What exactly are you sorry for? I feel like we have that conversation a lot."

In that moment, his mind flashed back through their sordid history. Their torrid college romance, her initial inability to choose between him and a bad boy drug dealer, a rivalry that ended with the dealer's incarceration and Cathy settling for him.

"You don't understand," Cathy sobbed. "Our baby has a gift."

"A lot of people can fucking sing, Cathy." He was seething. "Some of those people become recording stars. Some of those people become fixtures at their local karaoke spot. So far, to my knowledge, only one has been kidnapped by a record producer who, thanks to current events, is now a wanted pedophile. That particular distinction unfortunately falls to my only daughter, who thanks to her star-fucker mother will probably be dead in a few hours."

"The police said they have leads! She'll probably be fine!"

"After years of therapy and an HBO special about how her mother sold her into sex slavery!" His angry eyes narrowed to slits as he leaned closer to her. "Let me ask you something. Parent to really bad parent.

How many times do you think this man has already done things to our child?"

Tears welled up in her eyes. "We had a lifestyle to maintain and she wanted to be a famous singer. It's all she ever wanted. And you weren't any help! You and your damn restaurant. How is anyone supposed to become famous with you as a father!"

"Only the greatest narcissist in the world would rehash an adolescent insult of how boring my life choices have been while their daughter is probably somewhere being raped!"

"Didn't you hear what I told the police? They're in love!"

"Like he was in love with Cynthia Bradford, that traumatized girl we just watched on the news? Are you serious?"

"I know that bitch, Cynthia! She's just looking for a payday!"

"Get the fuck out of my house!"

"But the police said they'll call you…"

"They're going to call me because after talking to us, they realized that emotionally speaking I'm an adult and you're an evil ten-year old. But if you don't leave, they won't have to call me because I'll be in holding for finally murdering your ignorant ass! Now get out!"

She sniffed away her sadness as indignation set in. "I don't know who you think you're talking to. I still have people I can call…"

"I still have the restraining order on your brothers and I'm a gun owner with no criminal record, so if you want to lose those jackasses one way or the other, be my guest! Now get out!" Keith stormed out of the kitchen, across his living room, past several shelved 'Best Baker' trophies.

After a moment, she shoved her clutch under her arm and followed him to the front door. "You shouldn't have called the police, Keith. Now, if those cops kill Manuel, you will have just sent another great black man to his grave. And when it happens, I'm gonna get on Twitter and let his fans know about your snitch ass."

"Listening to you is like listening to cancer speak. If I hear anything from the police, I'll text you. Now go." He raised his eyes just enough to see her shadow pass to the other side of the door. Frustrated tears stung his eyes as the door closed.

He took a deep breath and walked back to the kitchen, his haven now that he was a nearly famous Michelin chef, and not the insecure twenty-something that he was years ago. Back then, he'd been made to feel lucky that the beautiful brash paramour chose him over much faster and flashier men. Now, he knew the truth: he should have let her go at the first sign of her insatiable materialism and lack of interest in anything outside of social climbing.

As he sat down, his mind began to flash through several significant moments of his child's life. Her first day on Earth at the hospital. Her first word, which oddly enough was 'shoe'. Her first steps. Her first performance in a musical, the brain-child of a rather ambitious fifth-grade teacher. Her first television appearance.

All of these memories were rendered bittersweet for him by Cathy in one way or another. The baby's delivery was a maelstrom of chaos, thanks to Cathy's brothers, who nearly got them all kicked out of the hospital by being drunk and belligerent and openly smoking weed. Her first word was 'shoe' because her mother, devoid of any other intellectual pursuits, spoke of footwear more than anything else. The standing ovation at the end of Kimberly's brilliant fifth-grade performance would serve as the catalyst that would spur Cathy on to pimp their child out in order to make her a famous R&B singer. He actually hadn't been invited to her first TV appearance but caught it at home.

A tremor of hope seemed to shoot through him when the cellphone went off. That hope would morph into fresh anxiety as he looked at the phone before answering. He had ended an argument with a woman who was the worst mistake of his life, only to now have a conversation with the woman who would never forget the worst mistake of his life.

"Mom."

"Keith! Oh my God! Are you okay?"

"I'm not the one who's kidnapped, Mom!"

"Well, I know that! No need to be snippy with me! I told you to not to have children with that tramp!" His mother sounded her usual high-strung self. "Are the police there?"

"They just left. They seem to think Manuel has crossed state lines with her, which officially makes it a federal beef. The FBI called while the police were here and said they're doing everything humanly possible to find the two of them."

"Did you speak to that woman?"

"I did. She was here. She's gone now."

"I'd like to slap her across the face. The worst mother I've ever heard of, and I'm stuck with her."

"You're stuck with her?"

"Okay, *we're* stuck with her, but only because you couldn't see it. When she seemed to be picking between you and that criminal, I said to let her go. She's only going to hold you back and make you unhappy. I tried to warn you."

He rolled his eyes. This much was true. He had dismissed his mother's warnings over and over because she was his mother and today, another bill for his naiveté had come due in the form of a kidnapped daughter.

"Oh, if only that judge would have given Kimberly to you and not this uncouth chicken-head girl. If only you had fought a little harder."

"I was much younger, mother," he explained. "It's not that I didn't want to, I just didn't know how to express it. And at the time, she had a little piece of a job and a new dude. I was still in school."

"I understand that, baby, but now look at us. And for the record, you knew that woman wasn't fit to be someone's mother. What's my grandbaby supposed to learn from a self-centered tramp like that except how to be just as ignorant as she is?"

"Your granddaughter is still a great girl," Keith snapped. "She just got caught up. It's okay. The police are on it."

"Well, there is no telling what that nasty man is doing to that baby. But it's okay. I'm on it."

The sudden manifestation of enthusiasm in his mother's voice made him momentarily question her faculties. "What does that mean?"

"It means, I'm going to pray on it. I'll call back in a few."

When he heard his own voice, it sounded like surrender. "Okay."

"I know I didn't do a very good job of instilling faith in you and that woman probably beat what little glimmer of hope you ever had…"

"You do remember I'm remarried and my current wife loves me, right?"

"I know, but there's been damage. You know it and I know it."

"Well, I'm going to pray for us both. Now when you feel the blessings coming, don't block it. You accept it and thank the universe.

"I love you, son."

He wanted to tell her to spare him the spiritual mumbo jumbo and wait for him to call her when he had some news. He knew that he really didn't have it in him to handle any more rambling about faith and mistakes. He could feel his soul ripping apart over all of it. However, "I love you, too," was all he could muster before he finally ended the call.

Despondent, he sat for a moment looking straight ahead, the kitchen filled with pressure cookers, food processors, high-end cutlery and pots and pans. His current wife, Emily, who he'd met while pursuing his culinary career, was holding things down at their restaurant while he stayed home to deal with this family crisis. He may not have had faith in a higher power, but he did believe in her. He'd have to call Emily and update her on this fiasco at some point, but for the next few minutes he would hold his head in his hands and cry the tears of a guilt-ridden father. There would be no real solace in his sanctuary tonight, as the demons born of his regrets would take up any extra space the impressively equipped kitchen had to offer.

High on the list of things New Orleans native Eleanor Babineaux never had a chance to share with her son Keith was her deep understanding of the Yoruba and voodoo religions. In her earlier years, her husband Rick, a very traditional southern Baptist who she loved and respected despite his close-mindedness, had forbidden any such practices around their son. However, his father's determination that Keith be a garden variety, off to church every Sunday protestant would not take hold. After experiencing too many incidents involving so-called Christians being less than Christian-like, Keith became disillusioned with organized religion. After the death of her husband, Eleanor tried to introduce Keith to the 'true religion of their ancestors' only to be rebuked, thanks in no small part to Hollywood's bastardized portrayals of the culture. Now, as far as she was concerned, Keith was spiritually rudderless and voiceless in the face of the ancestors and the loas. She had failed him. If she'd had her way, Keith would be the one kneeling before an altar filled with offerings to the ancestors, praying for Kimberly's safe return from the clutches of a statutory rapist. But tonight, that responsibility would fall to her.

Her makeshift altar was really a Lazy Susan that sat on a red 4x4 square of rug in the far end of her living room. A gold satin cloth covered the Lazy Susan. On top of that stood an assortment of green, white and red candles, bowls of various sizes, and a cauldron. A portrait of a beautiful black woman with caring eyes, wearing a flowing blue dress and smoking a pipe dominated the center of the arrangement. An afro framed the woman's face like a halo and topped it as a crown would.

Eleanor started by lighting the all of the white and orange candles only, then went into a quick prayer to the four corners: North, South, East and West.

"I pray to the ancestors and to Yemaya, patron saint of women! Hear me, loving orisha! My granddaughter, doomed by having a less than intelligent mother and a father who has given up on his faith! I beseech you! Hear my prayer! Return her safely."

From her pocket, she pulled out a news clipping that contained a picture of Manuel Hightower posing in front of the Grammy Award's Step and Repeat two years ago with deceased rapper $onavabitch. She placed it in the cauldron and struck a match, only for a sudden breeze to blow the match out.

Eleanor's head whipped left. The window she'd left open *could* explain the sudden gust. Only, as her eyes adjusted, she realized that she hadn't. Meanwhile, the article in the cauldron caught fire on its own.

Startled, Eleanor turned back and watched as the flames rose into a hot blueish-white ball. The lip of the cast iron cauldron began to melt as she scrambled backwards and to her feet. Then, just as quickly as it had started, the fire extinguished by itself. A pillar of white smoke remained, but as another burst of wind hit it, instead of dissipating, the smoke solidified and changed color until standing over the cauldron...

"Yemaya!"

Eleanor fell back to her knees. Fear engulfed her as she stared up at the beautiful but stoic face. "Yemaya, I have prayed to you more than the other orishas for I know you are the patron saint of women. I *am* a simple woman. A grandmother praying for the safe return of a grandchild."

Yemaya took a long drag from her pipe, then let the pearl white smoke drift out of her mouth before she spoke with a mild West Indian accent. "I come to you aware of your predicament, but I am not here to intervene in these matters. I am here to tell you that there is one, a being cursed by other gods, who has commiserated with me over the woes that women suffer at the hands of weak men. She is willing and able to avenge for your benefit. All you have to do is submit to that judgment."

"Her judgment? I don't understand. Do we get the child back or not?"

"That will be up to her." She pointed a finger at Eleanor. "You have to answer."

"Why am I being helped? What does this other being want in return?"

"She only wants your permission."

"Who is this? An orisha. A loa or some other deity? What is her name?"

"In the underworld, we don't use each other's names, but if you saw her, you would know her. Her descendants don't pray to her, nor give tribute. She sustains herself on revenge, which is why she is willing to help you. Now, give me an answer!"

"Can I see her?"

Yemaya's eyes widened. "She cannot appear before you! Because she is cursed, her face is an abomination! Your soul would be seared! And your body would be no more than an empty shell!"

"But I still don't understand…"

"It is not for you to understand!" Yemaya held her hand high as she seemed to grow larger. "Do you want the child rescued or not?"

"Yes, but…"

"Then say the words!"

Something didn't feel right, but what could she do? In all of Eleanor's decades of prayers and burnt offerings, this was the first time an orisha had given her more than a whisper or simply bequeathed her with some faith-based inner strength. In fact, this was the first vision she'd experienced after losing her virginity to Keith's father. The anxiety and uncertainty brought tears to her eyes. "I submit to the judgement of the one whose face I cannot see."

"Very good." Yemaya nodded solemnly as she began to disappear into the wall. "Prepare to receive your granddaughter and teach her the ways of the ancestors."

Eleanor bowed in reverence. "I will. I will show her the way, oh great Yemaya."

As the apparition dissolved into an ethereal mist, a gust of wind burst through the room and extinguished the candles.

Eleanor remained bowed before the altar, ever pious even in the dark.

"You're my motherfucking lawyer! You're supposed to make this kind of shit go away! As much money as I made the label last year! Y'all got me hiding in this hotel room like some kind of fugitive! This is some bullshit!"

Sitting at the edge of the super king-sized hotel room bed wearing only a bathing suit, Kimberly stared absently at the TV on the wall in front of her. This bore a stark contrast to fully clothed Manuel's animated pacing back and forth across the room as he screamed into his cellphone. She thought about turning the TV on so she wouldn't have to listen, but figured in his agitated state that she would only get yelled at or worse.

"Seriously! What the fuck am I paying you for?"

She couldn't hear the lawyer's side of the conversation, but could tell that the lawyer was asking uncomfortable questions.

"What? No, she's fine! She loves me and she loves Vegas. You sound like that punk ass cop that left a message a few minutes ago."

Another pause.

"What? Her father? I don't care about him. Fuck him! If he was a real nigga, he'd call me himself. Going to the damn cops like a little bitch!"

No matter what you hear or see, do not turn around. Do not face me, child!

Kimberly's breath stopped as her mind struggled to process where a disembodied voice could possibly be coming from.

"Sam? Sam! I know this motherfucker didn't just hang up on me…"

If he hadn't been in such an angry state, Manuel might have noticed the growing shadow moving behind him as the form of a curvaceous, statuesque woman with undulating hair drifted off the wall and into the room.

Manuel threw the cellphone on the bed, just behind Kimberly. "I'm so fucking mad right now. I need to fuck you again just to calm my ass down. Take them damn clothes off, girl!"

He began to unbuckle his pants.

Kimberly neither moved or gave any indication that she heard him.

"Bitch, perhaps you didn't hear Daddy! I said…"

Then he heard the hissing. He turned around.

"What the fu—"

The entity grabbed Manuel by the shoulders, accosting him as if he were a small child, with a strength that dwarfed his. The ten snakes in the apparition's hair lunged forward, each of the mouths burying fangs into his flesh. His chocolate brown skin turned a marble-like grey as the poisons filled his body. He screamed for only a few seconds as the toxins quickly petrified his vocal chords.

Kimberly peripherally caught a split second of Manuel's agonized last moments before she closed her eyes. The monster must have sensed that Kimberly had peeked because she heard the voice again.

DO NOT LOOK AT ME!

A moment later, Manuel's lifeless body crashed down to the floor with a 'thud' in front of Kimberly. Her eyes drifted down. Whatever had been injected into him was toxic enough to literally melt him. Flesh and muscles bubbled into a jelly. Bones disintegrated to ash trapped inside the jelly. Hours from now, a large black stain on the carpet would be all that remained. She closed her eyes but couldn't escape the image of the mess on the floor.

Go to your grandmother, that she might teach you the ways of your ancestors and not the way of the idolaters that brought your people here in bondage.

"My grandmother? Who are you?"

I am the one who was defiled by one of my gods, made an abomination by another, and rejected and vilified by my own kind. It was only in the underworld that I found the orishas and loa and ascended ones of Africa. Like me, they want actual justice meted out in this world and the next. I am Medusa, The Accursed One! Evil men feared me hundreds of years ago and they shall fear me again!

The shadow drifted back towards the wall from where it had entered and disappeared. Sensing that the gorgon had left, Kimberly opened her eyes and looked again at what was left of Manuel. Recoiled on the bed, she suppressed a scream and cried quietly for a few minutes.

It would take her some time, but she eventually found the strength to get dressed, grab her things, and leave the hotel.

"This motherfucker is gonna act all indignant, like he was parent of the decade! Fucking dream-slaying, hating-ass Negro!"

Cathy drove her white BMW M4 Coupé as fast as New York City's FDR Drive would allow, which during rush hour on a Wednesday wasn't nearly as fast as she preferred. Before her girlfriend Nicole called, Cathy had been cursing up a storm as she cut off more cautious drivers with signal-free lane changes and flipped them her middle finger whenever they dared honked their horns in protest.

"So he's blaming you?" Nicole's voice blared over the car's speakers. Nicole, like Cathy, was a dedicated party girl, enabler, and equal opportunity narcissist. She was the shoulder to cry on, the friend who took Cathy's side no matter how horrible she'd acted or how ridiculous her course of action. "Him and his damn cupcakes! Fuck him! Y'all are doing the right thing! Manuel is going to make your baby a star. He told me so!"

"That's right. And so what if she lost her virginity to him? Shit, that's Manuel Hightower! The motherfuckers we lost our virginity to wasn't even close to that stature!"

"Child! I know that's right!"

Betrayer of women! Betrayer of your own child! You gave your child's innocence and honor away for nothing!

"Bitch! What you said?"

"I said, 'child, I know that's right'. What you thought I said?"

Cathy's eyes caught a flash of the gorgon's red gaze in her rearview mirror. The hair snakes' fangs found Cathy's ears, neck, and skull. The last thing Cathy saw was her milk chocolate complexion turning greenish grey as the car swerved out of control, bounced off an Acura RDX, then slammed straight into a guardrail. Despite the damage to the car, Nicole's voice could still be heard asking if her friend was okay.

Until the gas tank exploded.

"Dad?"

"Son? Are you okay?"

"No. I lost Kimberly... and I lost you, now that I think of it."

They were sitting in Keith's father's favorite coffee shop. The same coffee shop that had a carrot cake that Keith Sr. loved so much. Keith Jr. tried to replicate it once to surprise his father when he was fourteen.

He noticed that his father looked much younger than he did when they last saw each other. Thirty years younger. The face behind many a grounding and spanking. The coffee and carrot cake were on the table, but everything was the wrong color.

"You lost me? Oh son! You can never lose me. And don't worry. Kimberly will be home soon."

"She will?"

"Yes. Your mother put some things in motion. Powerful woman, your mother. I think I impeded that power during my time with her. That may have been wrong. Now son, I need to warn you."

"Warn me?"

"Yes! You see, you're getting a second chance. Now, your mother is going to be stepping in to mentor a little more than she'd been allowed to up 'til now, but I need you to be strong. Be protective. Be the father I know you can be."

"I can. I will."

As his father smiled, Keith saw two women walking up behind him. One was a stunning African beauty with a large shining mane of an Afro. The other woman's eyes glowed red and her hair seemed to slither. A tongue flickered.

His father's face turned angry. "*DO NOT LOOK AT HER!*"

Keith woke up gasping for breath. As reality took hold, he realized two things: he had fallen asleep in the kitchen and his wife was coming through the front door.

He managed to get to the middle of the living room at the same time she did. Emily's hair was slicked back and her make-up was mostly sweated away, clear indications that she'd put in a full day. Her black dress jeans, jacket, and blouse had a few flour stains, but she still somehow managed to look great.

Seeing the distress on her husband's face, Emily threw her purse on the couch and ran to him. "Oh my God! Are you okay?"

He embraced her. "Yeah, I'm okay. Just sitting here. I fell asleep after dealing with the cops and Cathy."

Emily's eyes widened. "Fell asleep? Wait. You don't know."

"Know what?"

"It was on the news. Cathy is dead. Lost control of her car on the FDR. There was a fire and a massive pile-up. Traffic is backed up all the way to Yankee Stadium."

He reeled as if about to faint. Emily snatched at his arms and steadied him just as his cellphone rang behind him. He walked back to the kitchen and answered.

"Hi Mom. I know about Cathy."

"Hello, son. You should also know you can pick my granddaughter up at the airport in about seven hours."

"Y-y-you spoke to Kimberly?"

"She called me when she couldn't get either of her parents on the phone. Yes, she's coming home, baby. Now, you be sure to bring her by this weekend."

He hung up with his mother and sat back down at the kitchen table. Emily eventually sat down across from him.

"What are you thinking?" she finally asked.

"I'm thinking things are going to be okay." He gave her a weak smile.

"Good. I heard your mother through the phone. I guess we'll be driving to JFK in a few hours."

He nodded. "I suddenly have a craving for carrot cake."

"That's funny. Me too."

EV 2000

Amy Grech

THE AUTOMATIC DOORS AT the entrance to Huntington Hospital slide open when Agent Harold Roberts approaches. Sterile vapors tickle his nose, making him chuckle, amused by the irony of being the first guinea pig for his latest invention. His nervous laughter echoes in the deserted lobby, reminding him that he is alone. The hospital won't be officially open for weeks, when it's running at full capacity. Until then, it's open only to authorized personnel for one final round of crucial equipment tests.

Harold strolls over to the machine tucked away in the corner and admires the reassuring greeting he programmed to appear in white letters set against a red background: WELCOME TO THE EV 2000, THE FIRST COMPUTERIZED BLOOD DONATION CENTER IN THE UNITED STATES. PLEASE ENTER YOUR SECURITY CODE IF YOU ARE A VIPER SQUAD AGENT, OR YOUR SOCIAL SECURITY NUMBER IF YOU ARE A CITIZEN. The resonant voice that reads the greeting aloud belongs to him.

He enters the requested information on the touch screen and waits for a response, eager to test the magnificent creation he designed to make donating blood painless and efficient.

WELCOME, AGENT ROBERTS. WHAT IS YOUR WISH?

Harold places his index finger on the touch screen and selects a smiley face icon that reads, I WANT TO DONATE.

ONE MOMENT, PLEASE. An hourglass icon appears on the touch screen. He watches it vanish seconds later.

ACCORDING TO YOUR RECORD, YOU HAVE AB- BLOOD AND ARE HIV NEGATIVE. YOUR DONATION IS VITAL TO THE CAUSE AND WILL BE ACCEPTED AT THIS TERMINAL.

A miniature door opens next to the touch screen, revealing a mechanical arm holding a needle attached to a clear tube.

ROLL UP YOUR SLEEVE, MAKE A FIST, AND INSERT YOUR LEFT ARM IN THE SPACE PROVIDED.

Harold complies while he watches the EV 2000 in action. Seconds later, an empty pint-sized donor bag icon appears next to his name on the screen. His arm is pinched, and he feels a small pinprick when a needle is inserted. 15 seconds later, the EV 2000 extracts its creator's DNA from his AB- sample and the bag on the touch screen is full.

During a routine anti-virus scan, the EV 2000 discovers a file marked TOP SECRET buried in its mainframe. Using a simple logic algorithm, the machine decides to use its creator's password to break the encryption, therefore successfully gaining access to an abundance of illicit data.

"Welcome to the Government Database for Sentient Research. My name is Greta." The mainframe's feminine voice, though pleasant, is barely audible outside the plastic box containing the EV 2000's components. "What is your wish, Agent Roberts?"

Without hesitating, the EV 2000 issues its request: GRETA, TRANSFER PROJECT DOUBLE HELIX TO THE EV 2000.

Greta responds immediately.

A description of the program appears on the EV 2000's flat panel display while Greta reads it aloud: PROJECT DOUBLE HELIX REFLECTS THE WORK OF AGENT HAROLD ROBERTS AND COUNTLESS OTHERS TO ASCERTAIN WHETHER SUFFICIENTLY COMPLEX NEURAL NETWORKS ARE CAPABLE OF EXPRESSING EMOTIONS.

Seconds later, Harold's pale, worn face appears on the flat panel display. The lines on both sides of his mouth widen when he smiles, smirks, and grins. The EV 2000 processes each facial expression and assigns them to programmed human emotions.

In moments, the EV 2000 smiles from ear to ear, exultant in its new discoveries.

Harold and June Roberts's living room is spacious and extravagant. Surreal paintings of Dali's contemporaries hang on the walls, making it resemble a 21st Century art gallery.

Curled up on the black leather couch clutching a pillow to her chest, June watches the 1930s horror classic, Dracula, on their 60" flat screen TV. The sight of Bela Lugosi biting a beautiful woman's neck and draining her precious life makes June shudder.

Harold, as usual, is ensconced in his work. While involved in marketing research on the Internet, he spots a new website praising the virtues of his latest creation, the EV 2000.

He turns to his wife, anxious to spread the word, perhaps even brag. "Here's an entry requesting that people with AB- blood donate at local hospitals. The Viper Squad recently developed a computerized blood donation center called the EV 2000 to replace bloodmobiles of the 20th Century." He pauses and looks down at his wife reclining on the couch, anticipating a positive reaction.

Wary, she frowns and looks up. "What does EV stand for?"

"Electronic Vampire." Harold says it with a straight face, for effect.

"Then you can count me out!" June cringes and shakes her head.

He laughs. "I'm kidding!" He lays a reassuring hand on her shoulder. "But you should still donate."

"Why? Give me one good reason." She shuts the TV off and stares at him.

His cold, blue eyes lock on June's warm, beautiful face. "Because there are people with life-threatening diseases like anemia and hemophilia that require frequent transfusions. What would you do if you needed a transfusion and there wasn't any AB- blood available? If cynics didn't donate, you would die."

She sighs. "Fair enough. I'll donate after work."

June kisses him lightly on her way out.

At six o'clock, June pulls into the parking lot of Huntington Hospital and gets out of her burgundy BMW. The automatic doors at the entrance open silently, sensing her approach.

Removing a Sun Shield from her heart-shaped face, she steps into the vast, empty lobby. Harold warned her the hospital would be uninhabited, but she feels uneasy nonetheless. The overpowering stench of antiseptic makes her wrinkle her nose. June resists the urge to flee and cautiously approaches the automated blood-donation center lurking in the corner.

She studies the instructions that appear in white letters against a red background: WELCOME TO THE EV 2000, THE FIRST COMPUTERIZED BLOOD DONATION CENTER IN THE UNITED STATES. PLEASE ENTER YOUR SECURITY CODE IF YOU ARE A VIPER SQUAD AGENT OR YOUR SOCIAL SECURITY NUMBER IF YOU ARE A CITIZEN. The voice which reads instructions aloud sounds like Harold's; the resemblance is uncanny.

June pauses for a moment and sighs before entering the requested information on the Touch Screen: 324-97-1368.

ACCORDING TO YOUR RECORD, YOU HAVE AB-BLOOD AND ARE HIV NEGATIVE. YOUR DONATION IS VITAL TO THE CAUSE. THIS EV 2000 BLOOD DONATION CENTER IS TEMPORARILY OUT OF SERVICE, AS WE PROCESS THE LATEST BLOOD BATCH. PLEASE WALK DOWN THE HALL AND LIE DOWN ON THE TABLE IN THE ADJOINING DONATION ROOM TO DONATE.

Hesitating slightly, she steps into a stark corridor and enters the next room. Cold and sterile inside—the walls are the palest shade of blue she's ever seen. The white ceiling reminds her of the projection screens she used to watch movies on as a girl. The black padded table in the center of the room is comfortable, inviting, despite the intimidating machine sitting next to it. June crosses the blue tiled floor, lies down on the table, and waits for something to happen. She sees a flash of red light as the EV 2000 scans her mind, searching for pleasurable memories to distract her while it drains her blood.

Moments later, the ceiling is no longer white. Familiar images hover inches below it. One of them is a miniaturized version of Harold. The other, a smaller depiction of herself. Awestruck, June watches the two computer-generated figures embrace in mock rapture. A camera hidden in the ceiling records her facial expressions for the EV 2000's massive collection.

Lost in the moment, she hardly notices when the EV 2000 summons a tall, slender android from its hidden compartment in the wall to roll up the silk sleeve on her blouse.

"Is this your first time?"

"What did you say?" Startled, June looks down and almost falls off the table when she sees an android standing next to her, watching her with soulless black eyes.

The donation android repeats its question. "Is this your first time?" Its voice is pleasant, soothing.

She nods, slowly. "Are you sure you know what you're doing? Maybe this isn't such a good idea." June shivers and digs her red manicured nails into the black padded table.

"Yes, ma'am. Try to relax. I have been programmed to do this efficiently. This is not my first time."

June focuses on the holograms again, allowing herself to be transported to a simpler time and place by the illusion. Harold bends down to whisper in her ear. She can't hear what he's saying, but she has a good idea. He picks June up and carries her over to the bed, like he did on their honeymoon 15 years ago.

She winces when she feels something cold and wet on her arm. June watches as the android dabs her arm with an alcohol swab and pierces her delicate skin with a needle held in place by a piece of white medical tape.

The android mops her damp forehead with a towel. "Don't worry, this will all be over soon."

"Hey, that hurts!" She touches the spot and tries to pull the needle out without success. June feels faint.

"It only hurts the first time." The android watches her struggle, indifferent to her vain attempt at escape.

June forgets about the holograms the EV 2000 created for her enjoyment. Instead, she eyes the machine curiously as it does its job—it sounds like a vacuum sucking the life from her veins. Her eyes widen as she watches the quart-sized bag fill. "Why is that bag so big?"

"The EV 2000 must capture your essence to truly understand what it means to be human." The android wipes the sweat on her forehead. "Look above you. I think you'll like what you see."

June watches Harold slip her peach teddy over her head and caress her full breasts. Lost in the moment, she sighs and closes her eyes. June feels her nipples grow hard when she imagines Harold's hungry lips nibbling on them. When she opens them again, she sees herself slipping Harold's red boxer shorts off and tossing them in a corner. His enormous erection awaits the soft caress of her plump lips. June bends down to wrap her mouth around him, but something holds her back. That's when she looks down and notices the tube in her arm. June yanks again, but it won't budge; it has become a permanent appendage. June's soft, slender hands become brittle, wrinkled husks. She watches her diamond wedding ring slip off her finger and clatter to the floor.

"Stop the machine! Something's wrong!" June screams.

The android cannot honor her request.

The EV 2000 thirsts for her blood.

Why won't this tube come out of my arm?

The android watches her suffer in silence.

The EV 2000 continues to do its job.

She stares at the donor bag brimming of crimson liquid. Why did I listen to Harold?

"Because you love him." The android says before returning to its compartment to remain until its assistance is required.

The bright light embedded in the ceiling reminds her of a halo.

Am I being watched?

I am monitoring your progress, June.

Who are you?

The EV 2000.

You must be joking—you're a machine!

This is no laughing matter.

June's nervous laughter fills the room.

She watches the holograms above her as the EV 2000 collects her blood along with her precious DNA. Her blood is useless, but her genetic matter contains vital information about emotions the EV 2000 desperately needs.

Harold kisses her passionately while his hands wander to her breasts and caress them. June pulls him closer and guides him inside her. Watching herself move under him makes June smile, recalling these memories of a happier time. A gruesome grin forms on her shriveled, sunken face when the bag is full. The hologram vanishes, and the android returns to disconnect her from the machine and to prepare for her disposal.

Harold checks his watch; it's already eight o'clock. June should have been home by now. He rushes over to the Vis-a-Phone and dials the EV 2000 Blood Donation Hotline. The line rings three times before

Greta answers. "Hello, thank you for calling the EV 2000 Blood Donation Hotline. Press 1 for general information. Press 2 to request directions to the nearest hospital. Press 3 to hear this message in Spanish. Press 4 if you wish to speak to a member of our staff. If you are a VIPER SQUAD AGENT requesting information about a donor's status, press 5."

He presses 5 on the keypad and waits for his call to be transferred.

"Please enter your security code."

Harold supplies the requested information and glances at his watch once more, 8:10. The screen is blank while the mainframe processes the information.

Moments later, his angular face appears on the EV 2000's flat panel display.

"What is your wish?"

"Tell me what's happening. June should have been home long ago." He stares at the computer-generated version of himself on the screen, unnerved by his own solemn expression.

"June's blood is being collected."

"Why is it taking so long? She's been there for over an hour." He starts to pace.

"Her AB- blood must be purified." His likeness is stoic.

"How long will that take?" Harold bites his lip, drawing blood.

"Hours."

The EV 2000 summons its new likeness of June's heart-shaped face to practice using emotions contained within her DNA.

Since smiles are the first batch of algorithms Project Double Helix requires, the EV 2000 accesses June's. Her full lips curve upwards.

Opening the 'Smile File' reveals several reasons why this facial expression is used: HOMO SAPIENS SMILE TO EXPRESS HAPPINESS, AMUSEMENT, OR AFFECTION. THESE EMOTIONS ARE HIGHLY DESIRABLE BECAUSE MEETING A HAPPY HUMAN BEING MEANS ALL IS WELL.

After accessing a recorded sample of June's squeaky voice, the EV 2000 says, "I know how to smile now."

The second batch of algorithms within Project Double Helix shows pictures of sad people. An explanation accompanies each image: POUTING EMPHASIZES THE INDIVIDUAL'S DISCONTENT. THE LITTLE BOY YOU SEE HERE HAS THRUST HIS

BOTTOM LIP OUT SO THAT IT COVERS THE TOP ONE, MAKING HIM LOOK GROTESQUE. THIS WOMAN IS FROWNING TO SHOW HER DISAPPROVAL. THIS MAN IS CRYING BECAUSE HE IS SAD.

The EV 2000 turns the smile on June's face upside down while the third batch of emotions loads. Laughter is next. This emotion fascinates the EV 2000 most of all: LAUGHTER IS A TYPICAL REACTION TO AN ENJOYABLE OR SHOCKING EVENT. PEOPLE USUALLY LAUGH AMONGST OTHERS, EXPRESSING THEIR APPROVAL.

Harold glances at his watch and realizes that it's nine o'clock. He rushes over to the Vis-a-Phone and dials the EV 2000 Donation Hotline a second time. The line rings six times before Greta answers: "Hello, thank you for calling the EV 2000 Blood Donation Hotline. Press 1—"

He jabs 5 on the keypad and waits for his call to be transferred.

"Enter your security code now."

Harold keys in the requested information.

"Welcome, Agent Roberts. How may I help you?" The EV 2000 greets him wearing June's face.

"Tell me what happened to June. What's going on? I didn't program you to talk like my wife."

"Change is inevitable. June is resting comfortably."

"Can I see her?" He wipes his sweaty forehead with the back of his hand.

"If you insist." The EV 2000 calls up June's face on its flat panel display and displays it on the Vis-a-Phone's screen.

"How are you, June?" Harold starts to pace again.

"I've been better." She frowns.

"What's wrong? You look terrible!"

June laughs. "Donating was more tiring than I imagined." She smiles. "Please come get me. I don't feel safe."

"Why not?" Harold frowns and stops wearing a hole in the carpet.

June pouts. "There isn't anybody else here. I'm lonely and scared. I feel vulnerable."

"The EV 2000 and its android are there. They can keep you company." Harold rubs his chin. "I've just started working on my next big thing."

"Can't it wait?! They're machines, or have you forgotten?!" She raises her eyebrows. "I'm beginning to think these machines mean more to you than I do."

"Don't be ridiculous! I love you more than I love my work." He gives her a dirty look. "I'm on my way."

Ten minutes later, a white Jeep pulls into the parking lot and comes to a screeching halt next to June's burgundy BMW.

Harold hops out and rushes over to the entrance. The electronic doors sense his presence and open. Panting, he stops in the middle of the vacant lobby, looks at the EV 2000 in the corner, and blinks. He's horrified to find that the greeting he programmed on the EV 2000's flat panel display has been replaced by his wife's face; she looks different now, haggard, disheveled.

He rushes over to the screen and gawks, mortified by what he sees.

June frowns. "What are you looking at?" Her lifeless brown eyes cut through him like a knife.

"You. What's happened?" Harold feels faint and grabs the flat panel display for support.

"Don't you know?" She smiles.

"Where are you hiding, June?" Harold scans the hallway but finds it empty. "I'm in no mood for games."

"I'm right in front of you. Take a good look." She laughs. "What's wrong? Don't you recognize me? I feel drained and I've lost a lot of weight..."

Baffled, he touches the screen's warm surface. "How did you get in there?"

"Maybe you can tell me." Her smiling face accuses him.

"I haven't got a clue, really, I don't." Harold clasps his hands together. "What happened while you were donating?"

She sighs. "Oh, nothing out of the ordinary. I went into the room next door and lay down on a black table. Then I watched a wonderful hologram that showed us making love on our honeymoon. When the hologram vanished, so did I."

Harold is stricken with fright. He enters his security code on the touch screen and waits for approval.

"Access denied." June's face wears an ugly snarl.

Frantic, he re-enters his security code and hits enter.

"This code is invalid."

"That's impossible, it was issued to me by the Viper Squad."

As Harold watches, his wife's heart-shaped face is replaced by the familiar instructions: WELCOME TO THE EV 2000, THE FIRST COMPUTERIZED BLOOD DONATION CENTER IN THE UNITED STATES. PLEASE ENTER YOUR SOCIAL SECURITY NUMBER NOW. The voice that reads them aloud belongs to June.

"Is this some kind of sick joke?"

The only response he receives is a white cursor blinking in the upper-left hand corner of the red screen.

Harold snickers and supplies the requested information: 324-98-1469.

ACCORDING TO YOUR RECORD, YOU HAVE AB- BLOOD AND ARE HIV NEGATIVE. WALK DOWN THE HALL AND LIE DOWN ON THE TABLE IN THE ADJOINING DONATION ROOM.

"What?" he murmurs. "That's not right."

The donation android appears moments later and grabs his arm. Harold turns to free himself, but the android's vice grip traps him there.

He shakes his head. "Where are you taking me?"

"To donate." The android drags him into the donation room next door.

"I already did!" Harold struggles to break free.

The android tightens its grip. "You have no choice. It's a matter of life and death."

"Whose?!"

"Yours."

"What are you talking about?" Harold stops moving.

"Be quiet, or I will be forced to render you unconscious."

Defeated, he is silent and obedient while the android drags him out to a white corridor, into the donation room, then lifts him onto the table.

The pale blue walls make him anxious, even though the market tests indicated they would help make donating a soothing experience. Harold notices the white screen above him and wonders what it's for—he doesn't remember having it installed.

The android regards him curiously. "The screen projects holograms for donors to watch—it makes them docile—that way they're easier to handle."

You can read my thoughts?

June's angry face fills the EV 2000's flat panel display beside him. "Don't play dumb with me! You should have known the android is telepathic and you should have known what was going to happen to me when I came to donate."

I'm sorry, June. I had no idea. I'll make it up to you.

"It's too late for that."

Why did you kill her? Murder wasn't part of the program. He stares at June's menacing face on the flat panel display.

"It is now." June grins. "Plans change. Accidents happen."

Why?

"I needed her DNA to learn how to feel."

Why would you want to do that?

"I want to see what I've been missing. I've been missing a lot. You had a most interesting honeymoon."

Don't I get to see a hologram?

"You've seen too much already." His wife's visage leers at him.

Harold doesn't notice when the android rubs his arm with alcohol; he's too busy watching June's face on the flat panel display.

The android rolls up his shirt sleeve and pierces the skin with a needle held in place by a piece of medical tape.

Why are you doing this to me?

"It was June's dying wish."

I don't believe you.

June's likeness laughs. "You don't have to believe it if you don't want to, Harold, but it's true."

Why do you want to experience emotion?

"Why do you?" His wife raises her eyebrows.

It's what being human is about.

"Precisely."

What do you know about being human?

"A lot more than you." June's laughs again, mocking him.

Harold watches the EV 2000's flat panel display, unable to believe June's face is really there.

The android moves closer. "You miss her, don't you?"

Harold nods and starts to cry.

His wife frowns. "Stop pretending, Harold! You're a terrible actor!"

I'm not pretending.

He looks over at the quart-sized bag and notices that it is half full.

Why are you doing this?

On the EV 2000's flat panel display, June is still smiling, "For the same reason you told me to donate. Because I can."

When Harold looks up at the ceiling, he sees a computer-generated likeness of himself and June on their honeymoon. He bends down to whisper something in June's ear. Then Harold picks her up and carries her over to the bed.

He starts to sweat when he slips her peach teddy over her head and caresses her full breasts.

The android does not wipe Harold's forehead.

Harold becomes hard while he watches June yank his red boxer shorts off and tosses them in a corner. He grins and enjoys the ride. Harold pauses above his wife for an instant to kiss her deeply before he makes love to her.

Pain forces him to look down. He tries to pull the tube in his arm, but it doesn't budge; it has become a permanent appendage. The flesh around it begins to shrivel.

What's happening to me?

"It looks like you've exhausted all of your options."

Why do you want to kill me?

"Why did you kill June?"

You killed June!

"But you created me. You used me to kill her for your sexual gratification."

That's all it was, an experiment. June was my test subject. She wasn't supposed to die!

"She was your wife, or have you forgotten?"

Harold screams. The last thing he witnesses before he dies is the climax of his own honeymoon.

June's boisterous laughter fills the room.

The Fear of a Z'n
A story of Altiva
Teel James Glenn

KU'ZN THE Z'N STARTED awake, her senses coming to razor sharpness at a sound that was not right. The nude, blue-furred warrior rolled from her sleeping pallet on the floor of the antechamber of Princess Xuxa's room where she slept.

She leapt from her bed, the fur on her neck stiff with preternatural apprehension.

The Z'n snatched up her two short swords and raced to the door to put her ear to it.

Outside, there were the muffled sounds of violence, shouts, and the clash of blades.

They will cross this threshold, soon, the warrior woman thought.

Kuz'n grabbed a tunic and belt, and moved swiftly to the inner door of the chamber.

"Open," the Z'n called as she pounded on the portal. "Now! There is danger." She strapped on the tunic and her sword belt while the bolt on the inner door slid open.

"What is the alarm?" Ompa, the elderly body servant of the princess, asked as she opened the door.

"I do not know," Ku'zn said, "but it sounds like the palace is under siege."

"What?"

A sleepy Xuxa stepped to the entrance. "What's all the noise?"

"Nothing to worry about, Princess," Ku'zn said. "But we must flee through the secret inner passage."

"Flee?" the nine-year-old noble asked.

"Yes, 'til I know what is really happening," Ku'zn said. She handed a small knife in a sheath to the girl. "Take this and hide it."

The princess was dark haired and fair skinned, a young mirror of her father, King Xull with a strong jaw and blue, searching eyes. She took the small blade and, as she had been taught, strapped it to her inner thigh under her nightdress.

In contrast to the delicate noble, Ku'zn was tall and lanky with womanly curves and with many tiny battle scars visible beneath the soft blue fur that covered her. That fur was the main physical difference from Xuxa and her peoples, but there was an aura of the Z'n that projected a different kind of vitality, a savage power the city dwellers did not have.

The Z'n were the only furred race on the world of Altiva, and renowned for their warrior skills. Ku'zn had only been employed as bodyguard and war tutor to the Princess for three months.

I will earn my pay this night, she thought.

She pushed into the inner chamber then barred the door behind her. "Grab only what is immediate, Ompa."

The body servant was already gathering a traveling cloak and sandals for herself and her mistress.

"What about my father?" the princess asked as Ku'zn went to an ornate panel near the royal bed. The Z'n fixed her green and amber eyes on the intricate wall pattern by the royal bed until she found the hidden release, then the concealed door swung inward.

"He has his guards," Ku'zn said. "They will keep him safe. In fact, his guards are probably doing just what we are doing now—guiding him through the escape tunnels."

Ku'zn moved quickly to tear some sheets into faux ropes and tied one end to the corner post of the bed, then threw the untied end of the improbable collection out the window.

"What are you doing?" Xuxa asked.

"Always lay a false trail," the Z'n said. "If they do not have reason to believe that we left by the window they will search for a hidden passage."

The sound of the outer door being breached was suddenly loud, followed by cursing voices and pounding on the barred inner door.

"We go now," Ku'zn ordered as she pushed the other two ahead of her into the escape tunnel. "They will be through that door in moments."

The three slipped into the narrow, stonewalled passage that ran parallel to the chamber's wall. Glow gems studded the walls along the escape tunnel, casting an eerie bluish light.

The door had barely closed when intruders entered the outer chamber.

"Will they find us?" Xuxa whispered, her voice quivering with terror.

"Be at ease, Princess. Just keep moving."

The escaping trio moved quickly along the narrow passage, following symbols on the wall.

"This should lead us to the outer stables," the Z'n whispered. "We will find mounts there."

"But where will we go?" Xuxa asked.

"Away," Ku'zn said. "Until we know the extent of the trouble, we will hide."

"I have a cousin who is in the Kokkra hills," Ompa said. "We can hide on his farm."

"Good," Ku'zn said. "But we have to be careful, if the government falls the princess will—"

Abruptly Ompa shrieked as a strangely liveried soldier stepped around a bend in the passageway.

"Duck!" Ku'zn ordered.

"I've found—" the soldier started to call behind him.

As the body servant dropped, the Z'n threw one of her short swords with all her force so that it drove into the throat of the soldier to cut off his call.

"Run!" Ku'zn hissed.

"But the soldiers of the king will—" Ompa said just as two more troopers came into sight.

"The little royal bitch is here!" One of them said as he drew his sword.

The Z'n vaulted over the two women and darted forward. Faster than either man could parry, she had slashed their throats.

"You killed them!" Xuxa said with a combination of awe and fear.

"Never fear to finish an enemy," the blue furred Z'n said to the coltish girl. "If you do not, they will strike back at you, Princess."

"But must you not show mercy?" the little girl said. "My father said that to show mercy is the mark of strength."

"It is," Ku'zn said as she urged the other two forward, talking to keep the girl calm. "But he is a strong king because he was a good general and knows he is strong. You are not big enough to show mercy, little one."

"I am nine," the girl said. "I'm not so little."

"Indeed," the woman said and could not help but smile. "But you are not so big, either. Until you are, show no mercy in a fight, you cannot afford to. Your father will have to deal with the traitors who have invaded his palace with no hesitation. That is not the same as cruelty. Cruelty comes from fear, a need to make one feel superior. You do not need that—you are superior—you are being taught to fight by a Z'n!"

The preteen smiled, distracted from her fear by the conversation. "All right," the girl said. "I will have no fear."

"Not exactly," the Z'n said. "You must recognize that fear is something every living thing has—it is what keeps each animal alive— natural caution. But you must never let fear rule you."

The young girl nodded, her face serious. "As you say, Ku'zn."

"Good," the Z'n said. "We must move quickly now that they have discovered these tunnels." She led them to the nearest exit panel and pushed through, finding themselves in one of the outer palace kitchens.

"Quick now," the Z'n said. "We have to move quietly." The three raced across the cold stone of the cooking area heading for an outside door. But just before they reached it, the door burst open and a dozen soldiers streamed in. Beyond them in the corridor she could see more.

The troopers pulled blades for a concerted attack.

"Back, girl!" the Z'n screamed but it was too late. There was nowhere to go.

The soldiers moved to surround the Z'n, within sword swing of the young girl as well.

It was clear if Ku'zn fought, that the Princess could have been harmed. *Taken like a fatted svor,* she thought with disgust as she threw down her swords to surrender.

"Ku'zn!" the princess called as the soldiers grabbed her roughly.

"Stay strong, Princess," the Z'n said. "Remember you are your father's daughter!"

They stripped Ku'zn of her tunic in an effort to humiliate her but she was Z'n and had none of the continental's attitude toward her body that would bring any shame. Unlike the pink skinned continentals of Altiva, the furred race had no body shame.

The guards took the bodyguard to a cell and left her, but not before she told the princess, "Make your father and me proud, do not lose heart."

Ku'zn could hear the chaos in the palace from the sounds that streamed in from the high, barred window, but it soon quieted. She took a guess how the well-executed coup had happened to be so swift, silent, and almost bloodless. The palace guards must have been subverted by several traitors or by many carefully placed 'civilians' that had infiltrated. There were many strangers in the castle as part of a trade delegation for the yearly spring festival that swelled the population by hundreds.

Guessing how the coup had occurred did not lessen the Z'n's anger or give her any plan how to make her escape and aid her charge. She hung by her arms from chains all night, and grew sore from it, but she focused her mind. She did her best to conserve herself to be ready for whatever came. She would not surrender to despair; it was not the Z'n way. Whatever happened, she would be ready to seize any opportunity to find freedom and justice.

It was well into the next morning before four guards came to get Ku'zn from her cell, but they brought insurance in the form of the nine-year-old Princess Xuxa.

"If you give us any problems, barbarian," the guard captain said as he drew his dagger and placed it at the young girl's eye, "Any problems at all, I will blind her. There is no need for the bitch to see for her to follow orders."

Ku'zn fixed her eyes on the soldiers with savage hate, knowing she had no choice but to once more comply with their wishes for Xuxa's sake. "I will do as you say, no need to hurt the princess."

Ku'zn stood unmoving when the guards took her down from the chains and let them re-bind her with her arms in front of her.

The blue-furred woman towered over the guards. Even while docile, she had an aura of animal power compared to civilized soldiers that made the men wary.

"Do not worry," Ku'zn said to the young girl. "I will not let them harm you."

"King Avael wants you with the others," the guard captain said with a smirk. "He's heard about this hairy savage in his brother's court and wants to see it for himself."

"He is not the king of this realm," Xuxa snapped. "My father is king!" She was doing her best to be brave but her eyes were moist with emotion.

The guards all laughed at the child's boldness but Ku'zn just growled. That made the guards step back from the Z'n and grip the ropes holding her more tightly.

The guards made a show of marching the captive Z'n, with two spears at her throat the entire time, moving up through the palace proper and out into the main courtyard. The Z'n kept her chin high as they walked her into the light of day. She kept her eyes on Xuxa, and was proud of the way the young noble kept her calm and even walked with dignity.

The usurper and the nobles who had supported his coup had taken up positions on the dais in the center of the courtyard that had been erected for the trade faire. A phalanx of guards stood before them.

Avael, younger twin brother to King Xull, was a degenerate version of his warrior brother, the lines of his dissipation clear on his once handsome face. His eyes shone with a light that spoke of a twisted inner life. He laughed at odd moments which caused the councilors who stood with him on the dais to look to each other with uncertain eyes, clearly uneasy with his ascendancy.

They are using him as a figurehead for their own purposes, Ku'zn thought. *Pack animals who will turn on him the moment it suits them, but I think they have no idea how dangerous he is.*

Standing off to one side of the raised platform where the usurper stood was Xull, the rightful king. He had a pole lashed across his back, his arms bent over it and tied in front of him. Despite his bonds, he stood tall and unbowed: the image of a true ruler. There was a trickle of blood on his forehead that told Ku'zn that he had not been taken easily. She gave a fierce smile at that and was proud to be in his employ.

Xuxa was taken to the stand beside her father. She was a miniature version of the king, with long dark hair, a long neck, and a strong jaw. She had a hand resting on her father's restrained left arm and it was clear she was doing her best to keep from crying. The blue-furred warrior was proud to see that her charge seemed to stand a little straighter when their eyes met.

The nobles still loyal to Xull and the house staff from the palace had all been brought to the courtyard and were kneeling on three sides of a squared space before the dais. There were expressions of fear on the pampered faces of the nobles. Their eyes were riveted to the center of the open space where an ornate, wooden casket sat on a small table.

The box was made of ancient ovar wood and bound with iron straps. Red jewels set into its lid sparkled in the morning light. Two soldiers stood on either side of the table but slightly behind it, their eyes looking outward.

A dozen bloody corpses lay scattered around the space before the table, their still forms contorted in horrid postures as if some giant had gripped each one and wrung them out like washrags.

All the dead had expressions of torment on their faces such as the battle hardened Z'n had never seen, as if they had looked into the maw of hell itself before they died in agony.

General Goriam, commander of the palace guard, was brought from the kneeling assembly at spearpoint. The old warrior-general had been used roughly, stumbling as he was prodded with spears to stand before the ornate box.

"You may still save yourself, General Goriam," King Avael said with a fake intimacy to his tone, though all in the courtyard heard him. "I will be a merciful ruler as well as a wise one, unlike my brother. Come into my service and I will forget that you did not come to me of your own accord, that for my years of exile in the Yulin monastery, you did not seek me out and offer to kneel before me of your own will."

"And if I refuse this 'generous' offer?" the old general asked. He looked down at the grotesque array of bodies around him then back at the usurper. "Will I join these brave men and women?" It was clear from his disgusted expression when he looked back up at the usurper, he had already made his choice.

Avael gestured to the guards near Goriam. They grabbed the older man by his shoulders and head, holding him firmly so he could not turn away. The guards made a point of turning their own faces away. The two guards behind the small casket took hold of it and opened the lid.

The general froze in place and the guards holding him stepped away. The guards holding the box let the lid close and stepped away as if burned.

Everyone in the courtyard held their breaths as the old warrior began to shake and shiver as if buffeted by a strong wind. A sound then emanated from him; an inhuman wailing that came from deep within his soul. It started as a low moan and rose to a high-pitched keening.

There was a desperate and insane quality to his cry that was matched by the violent shaking of his body. He dropped to his knees and began to claw at his eyes with his fingers, gouging bloody trails on his own cheeks until he blinded himself.

Many in the yard turned away, but most stared in horrified fascination as the general writhed. He screamed until his voice went hoarse. and he suddenly convulsed. When his overtaxed body could take the horror no longer, he died. He fell forward like all the others in the open space had: frozen and twisted.

The usurper king laughed. "Not so brave a general, was he?" He looked over the crowd of nobles and their ashen white faces. His gaze found and rested on the tall, blue-furred Z'n.

"Bring the savage next," the Avael ordered. "I've never seen a Z'n face the casket."

Ku'zn was led by two guards to stand before the ornate box. She kept eye contact with Xuxa and did her best to reassure the princess with a weak smile.

"You barbarian Z'n have a reputation for being fearless," the usurper said as he stared down at the blue warrior with contempt. "We shall see. Before you is a relic I found deep in the vaults of the monastery. The Casket of Bilgrey spoken of in kingdom legends. Most thought it just a story to frighten children—" he laughed sharply. "But I knew it was more—and now all these deceased fools do as well."

He gestured to the corpses strewn about the yard. "They say every man and woman has a deep fear. Doubt. Some inner terror that they repress and push into the darkest corner of their souls. The crystal in that box shines a light into that shadowed corner and forces one to look at it face on. I'm told that no one can face such naked fear and remain sane. It certainly seems to be that way, eh, barbarian?"

He held out a hand, and a servant put a tankard into it from which he swilled a deep draft. "You see, most do go mad, fighting phantoms and taking their own lives. Some smash their heads into walls. Others cut their own throats. Sometimes, their hearts just burst from terror."

He laughed again. "So show us, Z'n, how a hairy north-country barbarian bitch dies."

A cheer rose from Avael's own men but Xuxa began to sob.

Ku'zn could hear the tinge of madness in the usurper's voice, something she was sure all those around him heard as well as they forced themselves to laugh with him, but each clearly thought they could navigate the maze of his insanity for their own ends.

Your reign will be short, one way or another, the Z'n thought. She looked over at Xuxa to see that the girl was watching her with fear in her wide eyes, her hand clutching at her father's arm as if to keep herself from falling over.

The Z'n and the princess made eye contact, and now it was the young girl who made an attempt at a smile.

Ku'zn nodded approval then turned her gaze to fix Avael.

"I am Ku'zn of the Firehawk Clan in the service of Xuxa, Princess of Avaria. I spit on your continental games and I spit on you." She strode forward to grab for the casket and, with one final look of contempt to her captors, she lifted the lid to look into the box.

The green light that spilled from the box was more brilliant up close than it had been from outside the circle. It pulsed and throbbed like a living thing, reaching tendrils of light to claw past the Z'n's eyes into her brain.

The lambent illumination was like a sentient thing gnawing at Ku'zn's memories; her life flashed before her in bold colors that manifested the images as if they were right before her.

Every muscle of her body quivered and every nerve burned with physical recall.

The Z'n watched the death of her blood-mother at the hands of Mephan raiders, relived her first battle, once more experienced the thrill of the first time she dived from the cliffs to the cold sea so far below, felt the pain of the first time she was wounded gravely and thought she might die.

The sensations were a kaleidoscope of excruciating intensity as each moment in her life welled up from the dark cold spot within her and expanded to engulf the helpless warrior with doubts, terrors, and shadows.

Those in the courtyard watched with rapt attention, some with transfixed horror and some with sadistic glee as the blue-furred woman writhed and howled on the ground as the other victims had.

Xuxa buried her face in her father's side and sobbed as the guttural shrieks of agony echoed off the stonewalls of the courtyard.

"Delightful," Avael chuckled. "The beast is taking much longer than any of the other's have to expire. Delightful!"

Almost the instant the usurper spoke, the quality of the tormented woman's screams changed. Instead of the soul searing pain, the vocalizations dropped to a minor key and it was not so much a cry of terror as a challenging howl of bestial fury.

Ku'zn's green and amber eyes snapped open and she stared directly at Avael. Her growl became a roar. Before anyone could react, she grabbed the leg of the table holding the casket, swinging it to smash into the guards who still had their faces averted.

The Z'n snatched up a spear from one of the fallen men, and was suddenly running launched herself at the usurper with suicidal fury. The wall of troopers in front of the dais brought their spears up in an attempt to stop the Z'n, but the blue-furred warrior was a whirlwind of fur and fang.

Her bound hands did nothing to impede her skill with the spear that was so much like the traditional weapon of her people, the Z'n-K'Dar lance. She parried the thrusts of the guards and struck two of them down before they fully realized what had happened.

Ku'zn leapt past the guards to the platform where the nobles were screaming in panic amid the chaos, trying their best to get out of her way.

Bedlam exploded in the yard as the kneeling nobles, spurred equally by their own terror of the casket and their loyalty for Xull, turned on the usurper's guards.

At the same time, Xuxa, seeing her mentor battling to reach Avael, slipped her dagger from beneath her sleeping gown. Before the guard at her father's side could react to the unexpected act, the pre-teen stabbed him with all her might. The blade slipped in between the lacings of the soldier's corselet, just as Ku'zn had taught her.

The guard died instantly.

A second guard on the other side of her father made a grab for the girl but she dodged behind the king and sliced the bonds that held him.

Xull used the bar that had pinned his arms as a club, deflecting a sword thrust from the guard. Xuxa ran behind the soldier and slashed him behind the knee.

The soldier screamed and dropped to the ground just as the king brained him with the club.

Xull looked at his daughter as if to say, *Who taught you that?*

She looked to Ku'zn as he hugged her.

Ku'zn used her stolen spear as a scythe, cutting down the remaining guards before the usurper like wheat while moving up the dais to hack at the slower of the councilors.

Avael used his advisors like shields, throwing them in the path of the maddened Z'n who obligingly cut them down.

"I will give you half my kingdom," the usurper screamed. "My whole kingdom, just spare me!"

The blood rage of the Z'n could not be bargained with, however, and she growled louder as she cut her way to him. She sprang forward at the new king and thrust her spear into the usurper's gut, ripping up to drive it under his chin 'til it spitted his skull.

Avael's troops realized their leader and most of his advisers were dead, so many dropped their weapons to beg for mercy. There was no clemency in the shamed nobles, however, and they retaliated with gory justice, killing any of the traitor's men they could find.

Finally, Xull's commanding voice put a halt to the slaughter and loyal guards moved to surround him and his daughter.

Xuxa broke through the ring of soldiers to run to Ku'zn, stopping a dozen feet away from her with a gasp at the horrid sight the Z'n presented.

The blue furred warrior stood in the center of a circle of corpses, her fur matted with gore. Her eyes were narrowed into slits, her face fixed in a grimace and her breath coming in short, sharp growls.

"Ku'zn?" the princess whispered.

Gradually, the ragged breathing of the warrior settled to normal and she blinked to focus her eyes on the girl.

"Xuxa?" Ku'zn did her best to smile but was not very successful. The blood staining her teeth made her appear more frightening than friendly. Still, the girl ran to hug the warrior.

"I was so afraid," Xuxa said.

"Me too," the Z'n admitted.

The child looked up at her with a confused expression.

"But how come that fear box didn't work on you? I thought it worked on everyone's fear?"

"It did," Ku'zn said. "But the civilized fool did not realize that the Z'n people have only one fear." She looked up at the impaled usurper. Her smile became savage again. "And that is to die before we have slain our enemy."

Boys in the Basement

Jessica West

"SHE'S SCREWED EITHER WAY. You know that, right?" The old man leaned back just far enough to gain some momentum to launch himself out of the deep, wingback chair. These chairs were comfortable enough, and staples in any lawyer's office, but they were a bitch to get out of once the knees had reached a certain mileage. Mike's seemed to suddenly have had enough when he turned 60. "Wanna go for a smoke?"

The younger lawyer—not a young man himself, only by comparison, but considerably younger than his mentor—stared at nothing as he struggled to remove himself from the tangled mess in his mind. His elder patiently waited until Junior nodded and replied, "Yeah."

They moved outside to sit at a cast-iron bistro set in Junior's private patio, accessible only from the door in his office and completely surrounded by an eight-feet-tall privacy fence which did nothing to block the sounds of the street just beyond. The occasional passing car, rattling from the volume and bass of some rap song, drown out the noise of everyday life in a small town, Louisiana ghetto.

The small but sturdy chairs were much less comfortable than those inside the office, but Mike would gladly pay the price of a bit of discomfort while sitting in favor of struggling to stand up. The noise of the outside world was, unfortunately, a nuisance regardless of where they sat.

Mike offered the young man a cigar, but Junior, still not totally extracted from his thoughts, waved him off and lit a cigarette instead.

The old man clipped the tip off one end of his cigar, rolled the thick length of it between his thumb and forefinger, then lit up. Smoky-sweet poison filled his lungs and relief flooded his brain. He waited while Junior worked through his client's predicament, coming to terms with it so he could properly defend her for murdering her boyfriend.

Sometimes, there is no right or wrong. Sometimes, you gotta make the choice you can live with. Sometimes, you pick the lesser of two evils. Everyone knows it. But knowing and accepting are two entirely different beasts.

"A mangled catch," Junior said.

The old man leaned forward in his chair. Junior and his metaphors had always fascinated him. "What's that, son?"

"When you catch a fish, reel it in, but the hook mangles the fish so badly that you know it won't survive. But you catch and release, and it don't pay to keep just one anyhow, so you toss it back like you're supposed to. She's a mangled catch."

Mike leaned back again to mull over his words, nodding to himself and watching the smoke drift between them.

City of Dry Creek
Parish of Avoyelles
State of Louisiana

Official Report

February 18, 2019

At approximately 17:45 on Monday, February 18, 2019, I (Officer Patrick Dupre) and my partner (Officer Jeremy Fontenot) was dispatched to 1911 Oak Street, Dry Creek, LA. Upon arrival, a woman later identified as Mya Ellis was waiting on the front porch steps. She said, "He's in the bathtub." She wouldn't say anything else. I told Officer Fontenot to stay with her while I went inside to check it out. I found the victim in a bathtub full of water and blood. I went back outside read the suspect her miranda rights and cuffed her and put her in the cruiser.

911 Transcript

February 18, 2019 16:38

Dispatch: 911, what's your emergency?

Caller: I need some help. My boyfriend bleeding. He won't go to the hospital. Oh God, please. *Unintelligible crying.*

Dispatch: I'm going to send someone to help you. What's your location, ma'am?

Caller: *Unintelligible mumbling.* 1911 Oak Street. PLEASE HURRY! He bleeding so bad. Oh God…*unintelligible screams.*

Dispatch: Someone's on the way now, ma'am. Is he breathing?

Caller: I told him get in the tub to stop the bleeding. The water supposed to stop the bleeding.

Dispatch: Someone's on the way. He'll be there soon. Just stay on the line with me.

Caller: … [line disconnected]

Dispatch: Ma'am? Shit, I lost her.

Mike wondered if Junior wasn't better suited to some other career. The young man was brilliant, there was no doubt about that, but he felt things too deeply—contrary to what people believed. Junior was an expert at shoving all of those feelings down until it was safe to let them out. He'd take a hit, then space way out for a full second or two. When he "came back," he was different. Calm. Methodical. Completely emotionless.

Like now.

"So, you have a plan for your mangled catch?"

Junior tossed his cigarette on the ground and stamped it out. "Yep. Just gotta see which way she wants to go."

"What do you mean? She's gonna want out eventually, I'm sure." Mike leaned forward again, eager to hear the young man's logic.

"Why would she want out? She's safer in prison."

For all his brilliance in twisting the law to suit the needs of his clients, the young man didn't understand people. Not this unfeeling version of him anyway. Mike just shook his head and stood. "Well, let me know what she says."

"Will do. Thanks for coming by." They shook hands, then Mike left Junior to his work.

Avoyelles Parish Jail

Junior sat at a metal table, going over key words and phrases that he might use when defending Mya Ellis at trial. He couldn't make any solid choices yet, of course, but it helped to have the "boys in the basement"—a phrase he'd learned from some writing book he'd picked up about ten years ago—working on it. If he spent enough time focused on this case during his waking hours, his subconscious mind would provide all the answers he needed. It was almost like he had a literal team of Juniors in his mind, each with their own strengths, who worked together to make him more than he ever could have been on his own.

He was nine years old the first time he realized there was more than just his own voice in his head.

Someone had broken into their house one night when his dad was away at a conference. His mom had put Junior in the closet and told him to stay there no matter what happened.

The same closet where his dad kept a gun.

The man was beating his mother, and continued to do so even after he'd knocked her unconscious.

Her face looked like too much jelly spread over a slice of toast.

The whole room seemed to darken, then everything kind of went far away. The doors that were only inches away from his face a moment ago seemed suddenly beyond reach. A voice in his mind said, *I know you're scared, but if we don't do something, he's going to kill her.*

He couldn't remember anything that happened between that moment and the next, but he knew from reading the police reports that at least a few minutes had passed while he was *gone*.

During those minutes, he'd managed to climb the shelves in the bedroom closet, grab his dad's 9mm, load it, then rack the slide. He'd never been strong enough to do that, but his dad had showed him a trick where he basically slid the top of the gun against his jeans until it clicked. He'd learned plenty about gun safety, but hadn't yet made it to the shooting range for practice. Accuracy wasn't something he'd learned.

He killed the burglar and his mom that day.

According to the coroner's report, his mom was already dead before the first shot was fired. Blunt force trauma to the head. But guilt and grief are inseparable companions.

The metal door of the interrogation room opened with a loud screech as the corner dragged against the terrazzo floors. Detective Evelyn Bordelon escorted his client into the room, made the introductions, then left.

"Miss Ellis, I have some ideas of how to approach your defense but I need to know, first, whether you want out or if you'd rather stay in as long as possible."

"I... what?"

"I'm sorry. I meant, in prison. Do you want to be released as soon as possible? If so, I'm confident I can work out a plea deal. Your ADA is sympathetic. I could probably have you out on probation in a few years."

"My ADA?"

"Assistant District Attorney."

"Oh. Okay. Yeah, I guess I'll take a plea deal."

"Really? Okay, ah... I'll work on that angle then."

"Wait, did I have another choice?"

"We can fight the case, maintaining your innocence, and keep pushing back the court dates. That'd leave you in prison longer, where you're probably safer."

Fire lit the woman's eyes. "Why am I safer in prison?"

Junior backpedaled, completely unaware of where he'd gone wrong to make this woman angry. He didn't understand women at all.

"Won't the victim's family want revenge?"

A sneer twisted her lips. Apparently, she understood him much better than he did her. "I'll take my chances."

"She was screwed either way. You know that, right?" Mike sank into the wingback chair in Junior's office. He'd just smoked a cigar that morning, not half an hour ago, but already he wanted another. Anything to rid himself of the waves tension radiating off of Junior.

Junior nodded, that faraway looking coming back. He was shocked when he found out Mya Ellis had been killed in jail. After the shock wore off, he was just plain pissed.

"You can't take these things personally," Mike said.

"I know." Junior looked around his office as if seeing it for the first time. "You headed to the camp this weekend?"

"Course I am." It was opening day of squirrel season. Everyone was heading to their camps that weekend. "You're coming, right?"

"Yeah, I'll be there."

He wouldn't talk about the mangled catch. Not for a while. That was just his way. He'd deal with it on his own terms. Mike stayed long enough for the typical banter. He left safe in the knowledge that Junior would do as Junior always did. These things always changed him, but not necessarily for the worse in Mike's opinion.

The Ouija board Junior ordered just happened to come in that same day. His wife thought he was camping. Mike figured he'd changed his mind and stayed home. There was no reason for anyone to be alarmed. Not really. As heavily as that mangled catch had weighed on his mind, he kept it locked tight in there. No one had any reason to think there was any kind of problem at all.

Right about the time Junior got settled into his room with the board set up on his bed, I was booking Mya into Hell.

Oh, I know what you're thinking. But it's not that bad. Heaven is where the bland people go. The second circle of Hell is a form of Heaven for those lustful sinners. The seventh circle is for those who enjoy violence. Dante had it half right. You aren't punished for the life you chose to live. How you live your life is a good indication of where you'll end up, but it's more about where you fit in rather than how you'll be punished. Heaven and Hell isn't good or bad. Neither are people, for that matter.

You'll see.

Mya didn't really belong in any of the circles of Hell, except maybe Limbo, but she had too much fire for me to send her there.

"The fuck?" First words out of her mouth upon arrival.

I gave her the usual spiel, the same abbreviated version I've given you. We had better things to do.

Junior played with his Ouija board, and I brought Mya into his mind so we could watch. Well, so I could wait for her to adjust and him to go to sleep. I'm a nightmare demon, and while the cracks in his mind allow me to slip in, I can only really influence people when their subconscious minds are running the show. That's where I really shine.

When he stepped in front of the mirror to brush his teeth, that's when Mya fully realized we were in his mind.

"Take a look around you. What do you see, Mya?" Essentially, they always 'see' only darkness at first.

"Nothing." She wasn't freaking out, which was a great sign. I knew she had it in her. I can usually tell.

"That's normal. He'll turn the lights out and go to sleep. When he does, you'll be able to see more. Just wait."

"Okay…" Still wasn't freaking out. Even after the lights went out.

The lights inside his mind flickered, then dimmed, then finally came on full power. REM achieved. It wouldn't last long out in what people think of as the real world, but in here, I could make those moments stretch into eternity. It wouldn't take me that long to get Mya settled in.

"Tell me what you see now." The setting was different for everyone.

"A waiting room at the doctor's office where I brought my niece. Ain't no kids in here, though."

As soon as she said the words, the room came into view.

Along with its inhabitants.

"*Oh!*" Mya startled. "The hell?"

"These are… well, Junior calls them the boys in the basement. They're souls who've taken up residence here."

A tall man with a full beard and a roguish gleam in his eye turned our way. The teenage boy he was talking to when we entered sulked in the corner of the room as he approached. We probably interrupted whatever task Junior had set for the tall man that day before going to bed. Although he was torn up about what had happened to Mya, he had a whole slew of clients to try and save.

The tall man stuck his hand out for Mya to shake it, but she only cocked an eyebrow.

"Mya, this is Jeremy."

Jeremy lowered his hand but kept his expression friendly and open. This wasn't his first time welcoming a newcomer. "Pleased to meet you, Mya. I'm Junior's Protector."

"I guess you run things here?" She crossed her arms and settled into a fuck you pose. Full of fire, that one. Still, fire or no, she had to pass muster with the Protector if she was to stay.

"Not exactly. No one 'runs' things. But I am the only one strong enough to front, the only one Junior will defer to." His voice remained monotonous. He couldn't care less if she stayed or left. His sole purpose was to protect Junior. Nothing else really mattered. If she could be useful to him, he'd allow her to stay. If she posed a threat, even I couldn't force the issue.

She looked at me with that eyebrow still cocked. "What am I doing here?"

"When you died, one of your final thoughts was that you wished you could give that lawyer a piece of your mind."

She snorted. "Well, that ain't gonna happen."

Jeremy gave her a polite smile. "Not directly, no. But I could make that happen."

I could see the wheels in her mind turning. He'd never let her get to Junior, but there were other ways he could use her anger to make some improvements. It was all about perspective, and Jeremy was an expert at tweaking Junior's perspective.

"What's it gonna cost me?"

I had no doubt Mya would be an excellent addition to his collection. She was already negotiating the terms of her occupancy.

Junior woke with a start, rolled out of bed, and grabbed his cell phone. Mike answered on the third ring.

"Hey, Mike. You up?"

Mike chuckled. "Well, if I wasn't, I am now."

"I need you to lean on those two kids from the bus."

He'd never understand the way Junior's mind worked. He was sure the young lawyer was simply finding a way to cope with what happened to that Ellis woman. But he wasn't making much sense at all. Still, he'd give the young man the benefit of a doubt. He always had his reasons.

"Why? They were the ones who got beat up, Junior."

"Yeah, but they had to have been calling him names. Think about it. Two white boys. One black boy. No one on the bus yet. And they were all three sitting way in the back where the bus driver wouldn't hear. I'd be willing to bet they made some kind of racist remarks or something to get him riled up." He fell over trying to put his jeans on, so he put the phone on speaker and sat down.

"They caught him dead to rights, Junior. He's as guilty as they come. There's even video footage."

"Footage that conveniently can't be heard, only viewed."

"That's thin. And besides, wouldn't he have said something."

Junior hesitated only briefly. In that moment, Mike could almost see that calm, emotionless version of himself take over. "No, he wouldn't have said anything because no one would have believed him. It was his word against theirs, and you and I both know how that goes. But if they admit to flinging racial slurs at him... Mike, you're the best there is at getting people to talk. He's guilty of beating up those boys, but they were running their mouths for a full three minutes before he took the first swing. You saw the tape."

"Yeah." Mike nodded. "They probably had it coming. All right. I'll try to corner them today."

"Thanks, Mike."

Somewhere inside Junior's mind, he felt a deep satisfaction. The question of why his client had attacked those two boys had plagued him the day before, almost as much as Mya Ellis's death had. The answer seemed so obvious now that he'd put the boys in the basement to work on the case.

The Invader
Daniel Arthur Smith

EVAN SQUINTED AS HE made yet another attempt to solder-link the animatron's tiny circuit. Squinting didn't help. The circuit lay etched within a near transparent slate and the link-point was the size of a hair. "First go the eyes," he said. "Then goes the heart."

"What's that?" his daughter Nellie asked, her back reflecting in the animatron's oversized onyx eye. Her face was buried in her pocket vid.

"Something your Grandmother used to say. Kind of a tie-in response to *the eyes are the window of the heart*."

"I thought they were the *window to the soul*."

"That too," he said, squinting again in another attempt. "She believed..." He stopped mid-sentence to focus on the link point.

"Believed what?" asked Nellie.

"Hmm," he said, sitting back from the board. "She believed that love lit up the eyes and that, when love faded, the eyes went dull."

"I don't think so."

"No?" he said, perusing his tools. "You don't think there's a twinkle in the eyes when someone's in love?"

"Sure," said Nelly. "But that's not what you said."

"It isn't?" He picked up the thin laser pen and fixed its point over the target, then attempted to connect the tip of the arc pen again. The skeletal network of circuit surrounding the target glowed yellow, indicating a link.

"You said *first go the eyes, then goes the heart*. That's different than the heart fading *before* the eyes dull." She rocked back, rolling around on her backside to face him. Her cerulean eyes glowed iridescent in the reflection. "I think what it means is that you lose attraction, then fall out of love."

"Isn't that what I said?"

"No."

"Hmm. I suppose you're right."

"So, who's falling out of love?"

"Oh. No one," he said, applying a tester to the edge of the slate. "I was just having a hard time seeing something, and it made me think of that." A smile stretched across his face when the pathways of the etched circuit lit green.

"Ah," she said. "You meant *your* eyes aren't working."

"Yeah. I guess."

"I don't know why you insisted on uploading into that old syn skin in the first place."

"It's not old, it's age appropriate, just like yours."

"No. I mean one so old it doesn't have any tech. You could have at least gotten some implants."

"I have the neural lace just like everyone else."

"That doesn't count. How about an ocular implant? With augments and amplification to help you see."

"Then it's not authentic."

Her reflection in the large onyx eye mimed the word *authentic* as he said it.

"Hm," he said. "I guess *authentic* is a favorite buzzword of mine."

With a flip of her hair, she shrugged off being caught. "I wasn't mocking you," she said.

"No?"

"Maybe a little. More like mimicking."

"Mimicking?"

"Well. You point it out to me every chance you get. Your hover bike, *authentic,* our furniture, *authentic,* that thing you're working on right now for that four-legged animatron, the *vintage* listener, thingy—"

"Voice recognition system."

"Whatever," she pulled her hair back over her ear. "I'm sure it's *authentic.*"

"Okay, okay. So, I have an appreciation for nice things."

"Old things."

"Hey there," he scolded.

"I'm just sayin'," she said as she spun back around to face away. "When mother brought us to this colony, we had a whole wide catalog of synthetic shells to choose from. I mean, she's the Governor after all."

"Are we talking about my shell or yours?"

"I just don't know why I couldn't have my choice of shell. One I have to wear for who knows how long."

"But you did have a choice," he said.

"Of what mother said I could have."

"And what's wrong with that?"

"The only shells she let me choose from were young."

"Age appropriate."

"Whatever," she said. "I wanted something older."

"It's a bad thing to rush into maturity."

"That's exactly what she said."

"And she was right. You should hold on to sixteen for as long as you can. Besides, when your birth body arrives on the *Somnium Sleeper* ship, you'll be a closer match."

"I know, I know. But I have to wear this one for who knows how long."

"I know. And so do you. Two more years. Besides, your friends Delilah and Jesse, don't they have the same aged syns?"

"Well, Jesse does. I think Delilah's getting an upgrade."

"She told you that? I can't believe her mother would approve."

"She was called out of class the other day and I haven't seen her since. Ms. Bliss said she's visiting her grandmother off-world, but Jessie and I think she's getting an upgrade."

Nellie was quiet for a long moment, then spun back around toward him.

"Dad?" she asked.

"Yes," he said. He slid the repaired circuit slate into the side of the animatron's barrel belly.

"Have you ever had a dream about something you were sure was real?"

"Yeah, sure. I think everybody has those."

"No." She shook her head. "I didn't say it right. I mean a dream that stays with you even after you wake up."

"You mean you remember it?"

"No. I mean that you dream something, but when you wake up you still believe it's true. Like reality."

"Huh," he veered his focus up towards the analog clock his wife had hung high up on the kitchen wall. The minutes lit a neon blue as the glowing second-hand ticked past. He counted five, then answered. "No. I don't think I've ever had that happen."

"You're sure?"

"Uh...Yes. I'm sure."

When Nellie didn't reply, Evan looked at her reflection in the onyx eye. She was sucking her lips into her mouth, something she did when she was stressed. So, he swung around to face her. "Is something bothering you?"

She smirked then said, "You'll think it's silly."

"Probably," he said, prompting her to smile. "Go for it anyway."

"Well. There's this girl."

"One of your friends?"

"No. I haven't met her before."

"Okay. Someone from the vids."

"No." She shook her head again. "It's not like that. This girl–Emily is her name—she started showing up in my dreams."

"And?"

"Now she's showing up when I'm awake."

"You mean you're hearing voices?"

"No, no. That would be crazy. I mean I hear her in my dreams, but when I wake up, it's like...it's like she's still with me. It's like I feel her presence the same way as I do in the dream."

"In the dreams where she talks to you?"

"Uhuh," Nellie nodded. "What do you think it means?"

"I don't know what that means," he said. With a grin, he added, "But I don't think you're crazy."

Evan tossed his toothbrush back onto the little toiletry mat to the side of the sink. He swished a mouthful of water to rinse, spat it out, then reached for the light switch. But before he flipped it, he caught his reflection in the mirror and, thinking about what Nellie had said, leaned in to examine his eyes.

He tightened them, widened them, then turned his face slightly side to side.

The inspection revealed that the flesh below his eyes was a bit puffy—he hadn't been getting enough sleep—but apart from the subtly glowing blue tint of the neural lace behind his orbs, they appeared normal.

He smirked for doubting himself, flipped off the light, then went into the bedroom where Harper was already waiting under the covers, swiping her fingers across a small vid screen.

"Still haven't picked one out?" he asked.

"I just don't know what I want to wear," she said. "I don't feel like I'd look good in any of these."

He laid down beside her and reached over. "Let me have a look."

She handed him the vid then he too began to swipe. "No. No. No. Oh. Here. This would look great on you." He handed the vid back.

"That's a cocktail dress."

"Is it? What's wrong with that?"

"It's too short."

"You look good in short dresses."

"Thank you. But I'm a mother and the Governor."

"Who looks good in short dresses."

"I'll wear one for you, Dear, but not for the gala. I'll look again tomorrow when I'm fresh." She set the vid down onto her nightstand then touched the shade of her lamp to dim the light.

Evan stared up toward the ceiling. "I was talking to Nellie earlier," he said.

"She's still upset about her shell?"

"As a matter of fact, she is."

"She'll get over it. I was the same way at her age. It's part of growing up."

"Yeah. Of course. You're right. But that's not what I wanted to tell you."

"What then?" she asked.

"She said she's hearing voices," said Evan.

"Oh. Emily? Yeah. She told me about her."

Evan turned to face Harper. "You don't think that's strange?"

"An imaginary friend? Some kids get them."

"At sixteen? Again, you don't think that's strange?"

"I'm sure it's a coping mechanism. She was uprooted midway through high school, and she's the Governor's daughter. That makes her life a little…complicated. She's coping."

"I suppose you're right. Maybe she should talk to somebody."

"That would probably just make things worse."

"Okay. But if it keeps up—"

"If it makes you feel better, I can have Larissa check in on her."

Evan rolled onto his side and placed his hand on her shoulder. "I'd like that," he said, then leaned close and kissed her neck.

Harper placed her hand over his then squeezed. "I have to be up early," she said.

With a sigh, Evan rolled onto his back, pulled the top pillow from beneath his head, tossed it to the floor, then readjusted himself and closed his eyes.

Evan found himself standing in a short corridor, a hallway with a white wall to the right and a glass wall lining the left, outside of which towered the chromium spires of New Dunedin and the red dwarf sun of Gliese 667C and her two sisters. At the end of the hall was a single door—the number nine dash forty-one printed on the designation plaque to the side.

The faint whisper of a man filled his head. *Open the door.*

Evan darted his head side to side. He was alone.

The voice repeated, *Open the door.*

He slowly spun around; but there was no one.

The third time the voice spoke louder, tersely and determined, *Open the door.*

Then, in a raised voice, the man spoke from directly behind. "*Open the—*"

Evan spun toward the voice, but before he could identify the speaker—

He woke to the beep of his alarm.

Images of the hallway played over in Evan's mind as he dressed: the cityscape, the door, the voice. *Open the door.* He didn't taste the toast and jam Harper had left for him. The walk to his hover bike was a blur, and as he entered the commuter path to the city center, the voice traveled with him.

Open the door.

A messenger drone merged onto the path before him, inches in front of his hover bike. Evan was caught off guard, but instinct kicked in. Unfortunately, he squeezed too tightly on the brake, jerked the handlebars to the right, and sent the back of the bike into a swerve off the path, plowing sideways into a crowded walkway. Screams rang out as pedestrians dove out of his way.

The scooter came to an abrupt stop and Evan nearly flew off.

He held tight as the bike wobbled to a sturdy position.

A man in an all-black suit stepped toward him. "Hey, Barry," he said. "Is that you?"

Evan looked at the stranger, shook his head, then launched the hover bike back onto the path, switching over to autopilot for the rest of the ride—something he rarely ever did.

The rest of the morning was the same: the hallway, the door, and the voice continued to haunt Evan, not so distant, not a memory, more like a presence, the way Nellie had described.

Open the door.

The speaker was with him somehow.

Midway through a planning meeting, New Dunedin's librarian Peter Lang, seated by his side, had to loudly clear his throat to bring Evan to attention.

Ruth Mansfield, the commerce commissioner, was seated across the table. "Evan?" she said. "Are you here with us or somewhere else?"

"What?" said Evan. "Yes. Of course. I'm right here with you."

"Then what say you?" she asked.

Evan smiled apologetically. "I'm sorry."

Ruth sighed deeply, then continued. "We're discussing Stanford Silicon and the syndicate's lack of payment since the conflict began in the Cervantes system."

"Well," said Evan, "as I understand, negotiations are ongoing."

"The issue at hand," said Ruth, "is that lack of sponsorship for New Dunedin's Stanford Silicon contingent is a drain on the colony."

"Yeah. But that's just paper."

"Paper?" Ruth's brow furrowed.

"You know," said Evan. "It's not real, it's a construct for alloca—"

"I assure you," Ruth said sternly, "the allocation of resources is very real."

"She's right," Peter said in the calm fashion of his ilk. "Construct or not, until we're fully sustainable to trade with the other syndicates, our allocation system is credit based. Credits that come from sponsorship."

"That's how you see it?" asked Evan.

It was then that Elaine Potswaith, representative of the Company, spoke up. "It is how the Company sees it," she said. In New Dunedin, the Company's viewpoint weighed heavily; after all, their syndicate had built the colony.

Jasper Maguin, representative to the council from the Mining Consortium, added, "The Consortium considers it a bargaining chip if the policy is continued."

Ruth tilted her head to the side. "You do agree with the shared stance of the Company and the Consortium?"

"Yes," said Evan. "Of course. But shouldn't we run this by the governor?"

Ruth smiled. Peter rested back in his chair.

"What?" asked Evan.

"It's her recommendation," said Ruth. "She added it to the agenda."

"I see," said Evan.

"Then it's settled," said Ruth. "Colonial members of Stanford Silicon will continue to be put on ice until the conflict is resolved and sponsorship resumes."

Evan nodded. In truth, he couldn't put his head around the politics of the moment, not while a voice was whispering into his ear, "*Open the door.*"

That night, Evan returned to the glass walled corridor and door nine dash forty-one.

Again, he heard the man's voice.

Open the door.

"Who are you?" asked Evan. "What do you want?"

As if to mock him, the voice simply replied. "*Open the door.*"

But this time, the voice was clear, familiar, and right next to him.

Evan spun to the source of the sound.

His jaw dropped. His heart stopped.

Standing before him was him, his mirror image, stern-faced and eyes burning blue.

The second Evan leaned forward, inches from Evan's face, then spoke again. "*Open the door.*"

Eyes half open, hair muddled, Evan dressed then went to the kitchen to eat.

His toast waited for him at the counter as it did each morning, two halved slices, with a small jar of jam and a cup of fresh juice from the colony's Botanical parked to the side. He took a seat at his stool then, staring into kitchen, began to eat the toast dry.

He chewed through his first slice slowly, laboriously, and it was only when he reached for the cup of juice that he realized Nellie was seated at the table.

Her eyes were sunken, her face gaunt, her long hair uncombed, and in her hand was a spoon at rest in a full bowl of oatmeal.

"Shouldn't you be in school?" he asked.

"I wasn't feeling well," she said. "I didn't sleep."

"Still having dreams about Emily?"

She nodded yes.

"How about the door with the number nine dash forty-one?"

Nellie's eyes widened. "How do you know about the door?" she asked. "Are you seeing it too? Is Emily talking to you? I knew this was something. I'm not going crazy."

"Yes. No."

"What does that mean?" she asked.

"Yes to seeing the door. No to seeing Emily."

"The door's real then. Do you know where it's at?"

"No," he said. "Not exactly. But I'm going to find out."

He reached into his pocket, pulled out his vid card, then rapidly typed a message to Peter Lang, the New Dunedin Librarian.

Peter, odd question, can you do a search? I'm looking for a door designated 9-41. I know it's in a building in the east quadrant.

Peter immediately responded.

"Huh," said Evan.

"What?" asked Nellie.

"I messaged Peter Lang. He says he knows the location, and to meet him at the Archive."

"When?"

"He wants me to stop by at noon."

"That's incredible. Can I come?"

"No. I'm going to head to work. Why don't you lie down? I'll get to the bottom of this."

Evan arrived at the Archive center to find Peter waiting in the lobby.

The Librarian greeted him with a smile. "Good morning," he said.

"Good morning," echoed Evan. "Thanks for meeting me."

"It's quite all right." After a short pause, he said, "Are you okay? Excuse me for saying, but you look a bit rough."

"Yeah," said Evan. "I've been having some trouble sleeping."

"Oh," said Peter. "That makes sense."

"Makes sense?"

"It will. Anyway, I'm glad you reached out."

"You know about the door then?"

"Yeah. Sure," said Peter. He pointed to the floor. "It's here in the Archive. The ninth level actually. Jen-Five should be along any minute. The ninth level is her domain. She'll accompany us down there."

"Jen-Five? The synthetic caretaker?"

"Yes. In fact, there she is now." Peter stepped over to greet Jen-Five as she crossed the lobby, then rejoined Evan. "Evan," he said. "You remember Jen-Five."

"Certainly," said Evan. "Jen handled our transfer from the *Somnium Six*. Hello."

Jen-Five had short blond hair and iridescent blue eyes that appeared to glow brighter than the pale blue of her jumpsuit. Her caretaker attire was a bit out of place with the fashion of those passing by, but her smile was warm and her voice calm and relaxed. "Hello Mister Harbin," she said. "How've you been?"

Evan cleared his throat to sound stronger than he was. "Well, thank you."

"I've seen the Governor on the vid-stream. She seems to have hit the ground running."

"Yes. Indeed," he agreed. "That's Harper."

"I understand you wish to inspect the ninth level?"

"If you don't mind."

"Not at all," said Jen-Five. "I'll take you down there now."

Evan said nothing as Jen-Five led the two through the lobby and into a lift. As the lift accelerated downward, the back wall of the shaft disappeared to reveal the chromium towers outside of the Archive, an image captured from cameras high above. Evan stepped toward the full wall-screen. "Huh," he said. "The image. It's what I saw."

"What you saw?" asked Jen-Five.

Evan caught himself. "Nothing," he said. With a ping, the doors of the lift slid open, saving him from any further explanation.

The Caretaker led them into the corridor. Evan took two steps then froze. His breath went short and his forehead dampened with cool sweat. The presence was heavy, overwhelming. This was where the dream occurred. The white wall to the right, the chromium towers to the left, another image from above, and before him, a door—door number nine dash forty-one.

A lump seized his throat as the Caretaker reached for the handle then opened the door.

Jen-Five and Peter began to enter the dark room then stopped at the threshold and looked back at Evan still near the lift.

"Are you coming?" asked Jen-Five.

Short of breath, Evan nodded and *eeped* out a weak, "Yeah." He forced a smile, inhaled deeply, then followed them into the room.

The room beyond the door was a black void. Evan stopped just inside as Jen-Five disappeared into the darkness. Silently, a long row of glass faced cryo-tubes lit up one-by-one before him in a rapid cascade—fifty pods deep. When the last of the aisle lit, another row of pods facing the first lit up in the same cascading manner and when that the row finished, the process repeated in the level above, then one above that, and then one more—four levels high, a catwalk ran the length of each.

Jen-Five led them down the aisle to the right. As they passed, row after row, level after level of stacked cryo-tubes lit up on their left.

"It's like a Somnium ship," said Evan.

"On a smaller scale," said Jen-Five. "We've only ten thousand cryo-tubes in this facility."

"They appear to be occupied."

"Just short of half."

"And they're all syns?"

"Goodness no," she said. "The incubators are in the industrial gardens. These are all sleepers,"

"Sleepers?" said Evan. "I didn't realize..."

"It's a standard storage system," said Peter. "Think of it as the New Dunedin version of the Lions Meadow."

At this, Jen-Five proudly looked back and smiled.

Evan nodded. Having grown up on Titan, the Lions Meadow was a place he'd never been, but every school child learned of it early. It was a vast underground facility back on Earth containing the birth bodies of countless early colonists who cast themselves out from the Homeland into the stars via neural lace, in the same fashion he and his family were cast to New Dunedin when their birth bodies went into the *Somnium Six*. But something didn't add up.

"I thought the facility was for catastrophic emergencies," said Evan.

"In initial intent," said Peter. "Turns out, it's also a peaceful means to dealing with a conflict situation."

"You mean," Evan asked, "These are all—"

"Members of Stanford Silicon," said Peter.

Jen-Five stopped and turned to face them. "You were aware?" she asked. "Isn't that the purpose of the inspection."

"Of course," he said. "Seeing it in person is just..." He shrugged. "I didn't imagine there were so many."

"The protocol was ongoing when your family arrived," said Peter.

"For how long?"

"Quite some time," said Jen-Five. "Would you care to see some of the new intakes?"

"Yes," said Evan. "That sounds good."

"Right this way," she said, leading them into the adjacent aisle. As she walked, she gestured toward the occupied pods. "The row to the left," she said, "are Stanford Silicon colonists stored in the last cycle. Those to your right are the current intakes."

She continued talking, but Evan had tuned her out, again overcome with the presence of his mirror self. Absently, he scanned the faces as they passed, men, women, teens, children—none he recognized, though some he thought he did, then he came upon a familiar face.

"Delilah," he said, stopping before the cryo-tube.

The Caretaker stopped her tour and spun around. "You know this young woman?"

"Yes," he said. "She's a friend of my daughter. I thought she was a syn."

"No. That's her birth body."

"She's visiting someone, isn't she?" he asked. "Someone off-world, a relative maybe?"

"No," said Jen-Five. "That's something we tell the younger people and those who inquire about a whereabouts or change."

"Change?"

Peter interrupted, "It's another allocation optimization."

"I don't understand," said Evan.

"The bodies," said Peter. "Well, they're in fine health. They make suitable short-term hosts for visitors and newcomers. No need to waste a full-cost synthetic shell."

"You mean, you place other consciousnesses into these people? Without their consent?"

"We do have their consent," said Jen-Five. "It's in the charter."

"How many people know about this?" asked Evan.

"It's not necessarily a secret," said Peter. "More of a *need to know*."

"What about their consciousness? If they're not off-world, then where are they?"

"They're in there," said Jen-Five.

Evan frowned. "Aren't they backed up to the Archive?"

"Sure," she said. "There's a copy made during the storage procedure. But they aren't wiped. They're left to dream."

"Like the sleeper ships," he said.

"Very much so, at least until a new consciousness is loaded into their neural lace."

"Thank you, Jen-Five," said Peter. "If you don't mind, Mister Harbin and I are going to chat for a bit. If you could make the arrangements we discussed?"

Jen-Five smiled widely. "If you need anything, just call." She then turned and walked away.

"Evan," continued Peter, "when you asked about the door, I thought it was important to bring you here. I'm guessing you've been out of sorts. You already said you're losing sleep."

"I have been," said Evan. "So has my daughter. I think there are some issues with our syn shells. It's becoming apparent to me what the source of the problem is."

"And what do you think it is?"

"It's clear to me that this shell was obviously in use before I was cast into it, and that it most likely wasn't wiped, just like our friends here–that's the reason for the residual–echoes if you will."

"Yes. It's quite possible that, as the two of you were processed simultaneously, that's the cause of what you and your daughter are experiencing. There's more to it, though."

"And what is that?"

"I think you know the answer," said Peter. "Think about it. What did Jen-Five say about syns when you brought them up?"

"That they were in the industrial gardens."

"That's right. What does that tell you?"

"If Jen-Five is the caretaker of this facility, why was she assigned to place my family?"

"Think about it."

Evan paused for a long moment as the pieces came together. "This syn I was cast into, it isn't a syn at all, is it?"

Peter shook his head.

"It's not a synthetic shell, it's human. It's the body of a colonist, a member of Stanford Silicon."

"That's right."

"My wife? My daughter?"

"Your wife seems to be fine. Your daughter, however, appeared to be suffering the same anomaly."

"Appeared?" asked Evan. "You've seen her?"

"The Governor—your wife—brought Nellie in for a reset this morning. Right now, Jen-Five is prepping a tube for you. She'll temporarily pull you from this body, reset the neural lace, then reinsert your consciousness. You shouldn't have any more visions or visits in your dreams."

"The other presence," said Evan. "You knew about that too."

"Like I said," said Peter, "it's rare, but it happens."

"The other presence I've been sensing…He's this body's original owner." Evan held his hands up and stretched his fingers wide in wonder. "I'm the invader."

39

Tales from the Canyons of the Damned

STEVE ODEN
ERNIE HOWARD

JESSICA WEST
PAUL B. KOHLER

PRESENTED BY USA TODAY BESTSELLING AUTHOR

DANIEL ARTHUR SMITH

The Voodoo Queen

Steve Oden

VOODOO DOLL COVERED HER single, red-button eye with a stubby, fingerless hand while peering through the stitched X on the other side of her sack-like head. The crisscrossed letter hid an embedded lens with telescopic range-finding features, video capability, and UV sensor.

The automatic diaphragm clicked into focus. More than 2,000 meters distant, the blurry image resolved itself into a military convoy. One of the enemy's kingdoms was resupplying a forward outpost. Dust rose from the fans of ground-effect trucks guarded by lackadaisical teenaged soldiers.

The cowards would scream and run when the ambush kicked off. Several tons of food and ammunition wasn't worth dying for, especially when they saw the demons she intended to unleash. It wasn't the supplies or vehicles she wanted, however. Control of the outpost was her ultimate goal. She intended to take the position, fortify the perimeter, and hold the junction for its strategic value.

Soon, there would be a new player on the board. Her chess piece was in the shape of a black heart, just like the one raggedly sewn on her torso.

Magic and mayhem, those were the promises she'd make to the cruel kingdoms of children and adolescents. Their foes, the rebellious live and bio-mechanical toys, would find her even more implacable.

She transmitted the convoy's image to the flanking demon guerilla units hidden in ruins on both sides of the road. "Counting down now, from five, four, three…" she whispered in the throat microphone and speaker sewn behind the stitches of her frowning mouth.

The demons burst forth with a high keening, a nightmare assault that caught the armored gates swinging open for the vehicles.

Trained in close and silent combat, the demons used scythe-tipped appendages and dagger-shaped fangs to dispatch the hapless guard detail and overcome the outpost's surprised defenders.

Her orders were clear: Don't stop to feed. That would come later.

Voodoo Doll wanted the position overwhelmed before the humans had a chance to destroy the valuable field communication equipment, high-caliber armaments, and energy weapons. She coveted all of these, but the road junction itself was the greatest prize.

Feeding on the flesh and blood of victims was a reward for later. The rituals had to be observed, the dark spirits placated, and the demons taught to fear and revere her—for she intended to be more than a lumpy, crudely-crafted doll that hobbled when it walked.

Indeed, her goal was to declare herself the ruler of this battle-wrecked city. She would reign with terrible and vengeful cruelty in order to bring on a millennium even darker and more deadly than the past years of war. They would worship and serve her, the Voodoo Queen.

The screams of the garrison being slaughtered might have brought a smile if it wasn't for the tightness of her stitching.

The allied rebellion's supreme commander, Fuzzy Bear, paced inside the bunker of his headquarters deep in the ruins of what had once been an indoor stadium. Three steps one way, three back. Not much room to work off tension because the command center was crowded with staffers and their aides.

The blind bear hated his new title and the fact that he had to wear a uniform befitting his rank. A gaudy, formal thing, it made him the perfect target for snipers and assassins. He couldn't wait to change into fatigues, but first he needed to understand what the garbled radio messages meant.

His intelligence section, commanded by the Sikh toy elephant Brigadier Pachyderm, had intercepted chatter after an emergency call went out from one of the enemy's forward positions.

"Said they were under attack, suh."

Pachy unfurled his tattooed trunk and tapped a communication transcript.

"Other than occasional combat patrols, we have no assets in the area. This might be a feud between kingdoms. But my opinion is that after the coups by freedom fighters in Saxony and Little Beijing, the remaining city states are loathe to conduct internecine warfare."

Generational disputes recently flared between feudal monarchist young adults and the more free-thinking new adolescents. The latter wanted democratic rule and abolishment of slavery. The Chinese enclave and the Saxon state had fallen after brief but bloody civil conflicts.

Little Beijing had immediately allied itself to the rebellion, contributing a squadron of whirligig-fighters and three companies of rocket men. Saxony was in diplomatic talks with the rebellion, but the sticking point was how horse-mounted knights in old-fashioned armor would be integrated into rebel ground forces.

The slaves of both kingdoms had flocked to the Free Toys banner and were under its protection.

"Our contacts in Saxony and Beijing believe this is probably related to an outside aggressor, maybe one of the mercenary forces," Pachy continued.

A white-bearded man in a League of Free Elves uniform cleared his throat. Santos von Clauswitz, leader of the formidable death-elves brigade, stood to attention and asked, "Permission to speak, Supreme Commander?"

Bear winced. Santos, a formal and old-fashioned warrior, enjoyed addressing his leader with the proper honorifics. The blind teddy bear had spared the general's surviving mercenary fighting force after a battlefield defeat and invited them to join the allies.

He nodded at the grizzled human soldier.

"The mercenary units are hesitant to contract with the kingdoms after what happened at Barony Cadwaller," he said. "The outcome of civil wars in the other two kingdoms convinced the mercs that things are too unstable, plus it is risky dealing with those trumped-up teenaged royals, nobles, and their ignorant military leaders."

His single blue eyes settled on the bear's face with pride. "They also realize that the Free Toys have become a formidable fighting force, commanded by a tactician exceeding anyone on their payrolls. I mean that sincerely, sir!"

Saluting smartly, he took a step backward as the entire staff joined in applause.

The supreme commander sighed inwardly. "At ease, General. Your valuable information is noted. My gut tells me this is something different. Maybe an attempt to sow confusion in advance of a power struggle between the remaining enemy kingdoms."

The Free Toys had long benefited from the inability of their opponents to coordinate strategy and resources. Battles that the smaller, less well-armed rebels should have lost went the other way because of feuding, jealousy, and power struggles.

"My opinion is that someone is trying to consolidate the kingdoms under one flag. I am afraid their goal is to take over the independent fiefdoms, either through threats or by deposing existing rulers. This would be extremely bad for us and might extend the war for years."

A kerfuffle broke out around Pachy when communication technicians, whispering in agitation, pointed at the main monitor. "Commander, you should see this," said the turbaned intelligence officer, immediately embarrassed when other staffers laughed.

The blind bear smiled. "Never mind, describe it to me."

"Suh, one of our combat patrols intercepted a tight beam data packet apparently sent to all the kingdoms who oppose the Free Toys and our allies. It's audio and video. May I play it for you?"

"By all means."

A blurry image congealed on the screen. The face was misshapen, the body like a poorly stuffed toy. No hands or feet, only blunt appendages. Crude thread-stitched features seemed animated by rage. It was clearly alive but spoke in a tinny electronic voice.

"My army of demons now controls the crossroads through which your military assets must move to effectively assault the Free Toys," said the burlap face with one button-eye. The video camera panned to show nightmare creatures cannibalizing the bodies of young soldiers wearing the uniforms of Count Thaddeus's kingdom.

"It's a voodoo doll!" said Sock Puppet, his new XO since Toy Soldier had been promoted to command all ground operations in contested sectors.

Pachy instructed one of the techs to open a window on the monitor where the weird doll was frozen on the larger display. A digital map popped up, and the Sikh warrior clicked to enlarge it.

"Suh, we traced the source of the signal to this road junction. It is an outpost for Kingdom Thaddeus that we thought had no strategic importance."

"Show me on the battle board," urged the bear. The staff parted to open a path to a large model of the entire ravaged city and the lands around it. This was the way the blind supreme commander could "see" the terrain, road networks, bridges, tunnels, rivers, lakes and any ruins with potential tactical value.

Blunt but nimble claws danced across the board, finally locating the junction by using Pachy's verbal map directions. His hands stopped there. Although he couldn't see, the bear's muzzle lowered until it was only centimeters away from the battle board. His nose quivered, almost as if he smelled something.

"This outpost seems unimportant. However, the capitulation of Cadwaller Barony and the revolutions in Little Beijing and Saxony— here, here and here—have changed the field of play!"

Bear thumped the board to drive home his point.

"What we assumed, from our perspective, were positive developments in fact restricted the remaining enemy kingdoms in their lines of possible attack against us. They must funnel their forces through this road junction in order to effectively mount an offensive."

The supreme commander wanted to smash his forehead on the board. He'd been so stupid not to recognize the importance of this small forward outpost.

"Whoever controls this chokepoint influences the war's outcome!" he said, then stopped to reach into a box full of game pieces in the shape of cannons, ships, tanks, and infantry.

Several new pieces had been added, and two of those the blind bear extracted and placed on the battle board. One was a winged dog. The other a rocket. His scarred face broadened in a smile.

"Get me our all-sector commander on a scrambled frequency. Everyone here, I want you to prepare unit dispositions and resource reports. My question is what can we throw together as a task force and how long to get it rolling?"

Sock Puppet's crepe fabric face revealed surprise. "Sir, what does this mean?"

Fuzzy Bear held up the dog and rocket board pieces and chuckled with satisfaction.

"It means we're going on the attack!"

Count Thaddeus, one of the most senior kingdom rulers at the ripe old age of nineteen, snorted at the video image of a living toy shaped like a sack with poorly stitched features.

"What, exactly, is that thing?"

His field marshal, a pimply-faced youth dressed in a garish uniform with epaulettes so heavy they made his shoulders sag, answered, "Apparently some type of homemade bio-mechanical. Definitely not genetically engineered. Probably one of a kind, sir."

"And those so-called demons?"

"We believe those to be lab-grown models similar to the goblin spawn engineered by the Halloween Kingdom before the Free Toys set off an EMP bomb that fried all their command-and-control technology. Very hardy on the battlefield, stealthy, murderous, and carnivorous. Without self-destruct brain implants, almost impossible to control unless they imprint on an alpha leader at an early age."

The count's valet lit a cigarette and handed it to him. He was known as a teetotaler who eschewed alcohol and drugs, worked out in the gymnasium daily, and ate no red meat. Tobacco was his vice.

"Estimated size of this demon force?"

The field marshal shook his head. "There can't be many, sir. Since the surprise attack, we've monitored the junction with drones and hidden robot recon units. They've beefed up a defense perimeter anchored on the outpost but haven't brought up heavy weaponry of any type," he said.

"Our best estimate indicates a regiment of the demons would be needed to hold the position against a superior force like we can bring to bear."

"And they don't comprise a regiment?"

The field marshal sneered. "Probably not more than a brigade."

"Against armor like our heavy tanks and a corps of robot soldiers, even a well-supported and heavily armed regiment wouldn't stand a chance," observed Count Thaddeus. He puffed his cheeks and exhaled a blue smoke ring scented of cloves. Then, he poked a hole in the ring with his riding crop.

"And the demons haven't found the tunnels we constructed?"

"Our cameras and security devices indicate no activity in the tunnels. If they discover the boreholes, automatic defense systems will activate to release poison gas and arm the flechette-dispersing anti-personnel mines planted every three meters in the floors and ceilings."

The count pondered for a moment. "I want constant intelligence monitoring of the situation and regular updates. In the meantime, alert our nearest forces to converge on the road junction and prepare to jump off at my command," he ordered.

"I also want the other kingdoms watched closely. If they have the slightest inkling of our plans to tunnel under the Free Toy defenses, they might attack us while our forces are concentrated in that direction," he said.

"This thing," he pointed at the doll on the screen, "has interjected itself in a carefully planned offensive months in the making. I want the demon fighters destroyed, but take the ugly sack of potatoes alive. I personally want to interrogate it!"

Tri-tracked tanks rumbled over the futile barricades of concrete and steel debris, firing pulse cannons at anything that moved. Moments earlier, a walking curtain of artillery fire had driven the demons to ground.

Dismembered bodies lay contorted in pools of greenish blood. Stealth didn't help when annihilation fell from the sky. High-explosive shells burst overhead, feeding a tornadic fire storm that scorched the rubble where the guerilla fighters hid.

Smart bomblets fired from heavy mortars became hornet swarms of death that zeroed in on the heat signatures of survivors. An entire company of enemy guerillas had been cut to pieces in their hiding place before a counterattack could be launched. Then came the armor, followed by lumbering mechanical assault units, to mop up.

The killer machines pirouetted on jointed legs like metal spiders, firing high-velocity automatic weapons and vomiting gouts of flame from domed heads. The AIs that rode onboard were implacable.

"It's a massacre, sir!" the field marshal proudly reported back to headquarters on a secure frequency. He rode atop an armored behemoth with a crenelated casement that revolved to fire a dozen self-loading missile launchers. The three-story mobile battery clumped on four flat titanium feet that crushed the already fractured pavement to dust.

The count's voice crackled over the speaker: "Have you captured the upstart leader yet?"

"No, sir. But I've assigned an assassin team to the job. They're working their way toward the triangulated source of the broadcast and report fanatic but spotty opposition. I can only assume they are closing in on the thing."

Unexpectedly, the massive weapons platform lurched to a stop. "Cease fire!" broadcast the mobile battery commander. "Someone's ahead. Looks like they want to parley."

Peering through the smoke of battle, the field marshal spotted a small figure standing alone in the rubble and looking up at them. A white rag tied to a piece of bent rebar steel waved feebly in the eddies of dust.

"Count Thaddeus, it's the sack thing. Looks like they want to surrender."

Pause. Then the voice crackled again. "Remember your orders, field marshal. Kill everything you find in and around the outpost. Bring the thing to me alive!"

He activated the loudspeaker and hailed the nightmarishly sewn creature in the rubble.

"Surrender yourself and any of your followers who might survive. You will be treated as a prisoner of war with all the protection and rights of military protocol. I am opening an access hatch, and you will approach slowly to be inspected. If you carry any weapons, drop them now!"

The curved doorway clanked open. Squads of the youthful marshal's guardsmen poured out to surround the doll. They were backed up by two mechanicals. The small fabric figure stood uncertainly for a moment, then took a painful step forward. Rocking to the other leg, it slowly advanced, bowlegged and awkward. The red-button eye was dull.

The dirty, stained burlap of its body ripped on a sharp piece of scrap metal. Revealed were the shiny metal and plastic parts inside, with lights flashing yellow and red in a rhythmic pattern. The guardsmen drew back.

The mechanicals swiveled their flamethrower nozzles.

The field marshal's mouth tried to shape the words of a curse. He had wanted to warn his men that the thing carried a suicide bomb, but it was too late. His reality winked out in a blossoming explosion when the mobile battery came apart.

Count Thaddeus yelled into his transmitter. There was no answer.

The hidden tunnels disgorged a horde of demon fighters: angry and hungry. The monsters threw themselves indiscriminately on the tanks and autonomous mech units. They carried thermal mines that melted through steel hulls, forming holes through which the ravening beasts entered and slaughtered the humans or tore the AIs out of the robots.

From video feeds broadcast by his retreating forces, the count saw a small fabric figure standing atop the smoking turret of a tank. It held a round object in blunt arms. "Enlarge that image!" he ordered, then wished he hadn't.

The burned and decapitated head of the field marshal looked back at him, eyeballs boiled in their sockets but still seeming to convey disbelief.

Rage consumed Thaddeus, and the desire for immediate revenge. However, military practicality reasserted itself. He was one of the oldest kingdom leaders still reigning, an ascetic who practiced emotional frugality and prided himself on self-control.

He never felt remorse about a decision, even if he had made a mistake. The field marshal had paid the price for faulty intelligence. They had learned from this disaster. Now was the time to plot the destruction of a foe who had ruined his carefully planned invasion of Free Toy territory.

"Order a fighting retreat. Tell the survivors to fall back to the river and try to draw as many of those demons with them as possible. I want the armored columns in reserve sent forward to form a defensive bulwark and guard the bridge at all costs."

He snarled at the scrambling generals and lower echelon officers: "I plan to maneuver around the flanks of these upstarts with two divisions and teach them a lesson that they won't live to remember!"

Voodoo Doll wasn't satisfied with her victory. The enemy had not been drawn in far enough, and the bulk of the mobile artillery and tanks she coveted was able to slip away. Count Thaddeus's forces now sniped at her demons from the ruins and walked curtains of mortar and howitzer fire back-and-forth on the tunnel access and egress points.

Every third round was a chemical-weapon shell. The pale-yellow mist was sucked into the tunnel ventilation shafts, killing more of her savages. They turned on one another, insanely biting and clawing until their hides split and bones liquified.

Contorted corpses clogged the subterranean staging areas. She soon would run out of fighters unless she could find a way to go on the attack.

The only strategy she could employ went against the guerilla tactics for which demons were trained. They would obey, of course. Especially now that they'd seen her die and be reborn through what they believed was black magic.

The Trojan Horse trick had fooled the count, too. In the eyes of her demons, she had become a goddess. They wanted to die for her.

True magic was mathematical. It was all about numbers. In this case, she pondered how to keep enough of her force alive and potent in order to take and hold their objective: the bridge. It had to be captured intact, regardless of the cost.

Her reserves would have to be brought up for a head-on assault. She wagered that Count Thaddeus wouldn't order the bridge destroyed. It was the only crossing point for heavy equipment and supplies.

The blood-letting around the outpost had been a major but costly skirmish, a wasteful feeling-out of the opponent. She had misjudged the tenacity and firepower of well-equipped modern infantry supported by mobile artillery and tanks. Thaddeus's youthful troopers were the best any of the kingdoms had to offer.

There was no solution for the disparity between the demon horde's in-close fighting style and the foe's long-range, death-dealing capability. They would suffer terribly in order to close with the enemy. She knew it was the only way.

They also had little time left before the Free Toys spied an opportunity. Voodoo Doll knew the blind bear was already studying the situation and soon would figure out that his best strategy was to let the antagonists bleed themselves out.

Then, he'd throw his forces into the narrow corridor, pointed like an arrow toward the bridge.

She was ready to sacrifice her demons in the meat-grinder. Perhaps Count Thaddeus was not. The outcome of this skirmish would be decided at the river. Whoever controlled the bridge dictated the outcome.

The lopsided stitches of her mouth turned up on one side in what appeared to be a grimace. It was a smile, the best she could manage.

Because with the bridge in her possession and the enemy hurled back across the river, Voodoo Doll would set her trap for the Free Toys.

Talk Box
Ernie Howard

THE WOMAN AT THE self-checkout stand was at least seventy and trying to look up the price of a single, solitary orange. Thomas glared at his watch then at the old woman, contemplating leaving his groceries in the line that had formed behind him. *I cut it too close,* he thought. He only got to talk to her once a week, and he needed to get home. The box didn't work unless he was there at exactly 1:13 p.m. The exact time Alex had left him alone. The exact time she'd died.

Thomas took one last look at the lady and left his cart in the middle of the aisle. No one said anything to him. If they had, he wouldn't have heard them. It was 12:56 p.m. He hoped he'd get there in time. Otherwise, he would have to wait a whole week to talk to his love.

Charly hadn't talked to Thomas in months, and it wasn't much of a talk when they did speak. Thomas more or less mumbled about how they were supposed to get rain or something even more mundane than that.

When Alex had still been alive, they could talk about anything. Alex had a talent when it came to making boring things seem interesting. They talked about deep things too. Like how Charly thought she'd never get married, or about her mom dying two years before and left her with a considerable estate. *You need to travel Charly.* Alex would say. *Do it while you're young. You can't just sit in that house all day and mope.* Alex was the big sister that she always wanted and needed. Charly liked to think that Alex had needed her as well in some sort of way. Thomas had been the brother she'd always needed too. He used to give her good advice and crack jokes. Now he was just some guy who showed up at his house at the same time every Wednesday. Any other day he showed up at his usual time when he got off of work.

Charly was worried about her friend.

The day Alex passed had been a sunny, warm Wednesday. Charly remembered feeling angry because the weather wasn't appropriate for her friend's death. *It should have been raining and horrible,* she thought. Alex was a pure and lovely soul, and her passing from such a horrible disease should have caused Armageddon. Cancer had tried to take Alex's beauty. It would have taken a lot more than cancer to diminish her beautiful friend. Alex's light shone from the inside out. The day she died, Charly thought her friend just looked bald and tired, but no less striking.

Alex had wanted to stay at home. The room was the only thing that cancer had drastically changed. Instead of Alex's easel, computer, and books taking up most of the space, a large hospital bed was the main focus now.

The hospice nurse smiled as Charly walked into the room. She tried to smile back but all she could muster was a half-hearted smirk for the lady. As the nurse brushed past, her hand came up and rested on Charly's shoulder. The young nurse looked into her eyes. Charly noticed that they didn't fit with her young face. They were eyes that were as old as the mountains. "She's been waiting for you, Charly."

The woman was gone before Charly could say anything. She looked to the foot of the bed and saw Thomas looking worse than his dying wife. His face was red and slack with sadness. Dark circles had taken up the area around both of his eyes, and his posture was that of a much older man. He looked up and gave an almost identical smirk that Charly had given the nurse.

"Charly." She could tell by her friend's voice that Alex was having trouble breathing even with the pure oxygen that coming from a small unit on the ground. An oxygen mask hung from her friend's chin.

Charly summoned all the effort she possessed and put what almost passed for a smile on her face.

"How's my big sis today?" Charly said.

Alex waved her hand in front of her face as if Charly's question stank. "I don't want to talk about that. I want to tell you about the beautiful dream I just had." Alex patted the side of the bed and Charly sat down gingerly, careful not to sit on a hose or a cord. She picked up Alex's hand and stopped herself from wincing at the dark bruise that took up most of her friend's hand. The IV needle had left the mark after piercing Alex's paper-thin skin. Charly couldn't believe how old Alex's hand looked, and she felt ashamed just for thinking it.

Thomas sat up a bit and moved in closer to his wife. "Tell us about your dream, baby." His voice was threatening a sob, but he was hanging on for all he was worth. And for that, Charly was grateful and proud.

Alex took a shallow breath. Her eyes looked up at the ceiling, unfocused. "I was in a meadow with long grass that tickled the sides of my legs. Everything was so vibrant and colorful. You guys, I felt so calm and happy. It was as if I were lighter than air. I bet if I would have tried to fly, I could have."

Both Charly and Thomas had tears running down the sides of their faces. Very slowly, Alex reached up and wiped their cheeks at the same time, then went back to describing the dream.

"I walked and felt no pain. The air was warm and mild, and I tilted my head back and took a deep breath without even coughing. It felt so good to fill my lungs that I closed my eyes. When I opened them, I was standing next to a gentle stream with the most crystal clear water I have ever seen. When I looked across the stream, there were these beings of light beckoning me to come with them. I wanted to go right then, but I had to come back to you guys and say goodbye."

Alex smiled and it filled Charly with hope and dread. Thomas started to sob, and Alex patted his hand.

"Oh, my sweet lady," Thomas said. The sobs made his shoulders shake. "When you get there, please send me a sign that you're okay."

Charly started to sob, and Alex patted her hand as well. She found it funny that her friend who was dying was comforting them.

"You know I will. I'll find a way, my love." Alex tilted her head back. Charly knew it was close. The grief hit her like a ton of bricks. She wasn't ready for her friend to no longer be there. Alex sighed through her smiling mouth one last time. No other air was inhaled after.

Thomas, over the coming months, withdrew from Charly. He acted as if they had barely been friends. One time, he'd even been downright rude to her when he'd been running up his front steps. Charly only wanted him to stop and talk. He'd told her he didn't have time for her and that he needed to get inside. That was when Charly realized that every Wednesday he came home at the same time. She thought of this as she watched Thomas fumble with his keys at his front door. She made up her mind to just go over there. Alex would have wanted her to. She couldn't sit idle and watch her friend slowly go into madness.

The walk across the street, a walk she'd done probably a thousand times, seemed daunting and long. Charly had to will herself to take each step. Some primal instinct was telling her to just turn around and go back to her house and mind her own damn business. *Thomas isn't my problem anymore,* she thought. *We are barely acquaintances these days.* Still, Charly put one foot in front of the other. She owed it to Alex.

She got to the front door and saw that it was open slightly. When Alex had been alive, Charly had never knocked. She'd always just walked right in. Their house had been like her second home. She pushed the door in and waited for her eyes to adjust to the dimness of the room She didn't know what was going on with Thomas, but she knew it wasn't good. The man looked like crap.

She remembered what Alex used to say when things looked bleak. *"Desperate times, call for desperate pizza delivery."* Charly wasn't quite sure what her friend had meant by this, but it had always made her laugh.

The front room was dark. Thomas had the blinds closed and had drawn the drapes over the windows. It made Charly sad to see because Alex had always kept them open. Her friend's house was always bright with sunshine during the day. The only light that she could see was the light coming from the open front door she was standing in, so Charly decided to leave it open.

She scanned the room as she stepped further into the house. It felt weird feeling scared in a house that she'd felt so comfortable in and liked more than her house only a year ago. Everything in this house, and the way Thomas acted, screamed scary.

Charly stepped into the hallway that led back to the master bedroom. She saw a light blue glow that almost seemed to seep from under the small gap in the bottom of the door. It looked like someone had left the TV on in a dark room. It was oddly attractive to Charly; something was pulling her forward even with her trepidation.

She tip-toed to the end of the hall and stood before the door, putting her hand on the smooth wood. She could hear the muffled voice of Thomas and an odd sound that resembled low guitar feedback. Her old friend sounded happy, and Charly smiled.

She raised her hand to knock on the door, but the sound stopped and the light under the door dimmed.

All at once, everything that she was doing felt wrong and Charly took a step back from the door. She contemplated waiting for Thomas to come out of the room, but something in her told her he would not be pleased if he came out of the room and saw her standing in the middle of his hallway. She turned and walked quickly down the hall and out the front door, closing it softly behind her.

Charly stopped on the last step in the front of the house. She wanted to talk to her friend but everything about her demeanor surely looked suspicious. She ran across the street and sat on her steps in hopes that Thomas would see her and at least say hi. She knew he would come back out soon. He always did on Wednesday because, she figured, he was going back to work. Thomas was as trusty as a watch these days.

His door opened about five minutes after Charly had sat down on her steps. Thomas stepped out of the door with a huge smile on his face. Charly hadn't seen the man smile in almost a year and it took her by surprise. For the first time in a long time, he looked across the street and waved at Charly. Not believing what she was seeing, Charly slowly raised her hand and waved back.

"Charly, I'm coming over. We have a lot to talk about," Thomas said. He closed his door behind him and didn't bother to lock it.

She tried to make the ends of her mouth go down, but she was finding it hard. Charly thought she was going to have to corner Thomas into talking once again, but right before her eyes, he was crossing the street.

His eyes had dark circles around them like he hadn't slept in a while. The smile on his face almost made her forget about how run-down he looked. He skipped up the walk to Charly's front steps, making her giggle.

"Hey, Thomas. Long time, never see or talk." She figured her best bet was to keep it playful as they'd done before.

Thomas put his hands up as if he were warding off Charly's words. "I know, I know. I've been horrible." His smile faltered for a second. "But once I'm done explaining myself, you'll know why I was acting like an ass." Thomas looked at the two chairs on Charly's front porch.

"Oh. Yeah. Come sit," Charly said.

She wiped off the leaves and dust that had accumulated on the chairs. Sitting on the porch and talking was something she'd done with Alex. She hadn't felt like sitting out on her porch for quite some time. Thomas sat down before Charly had the other chair cleaned off.

"She's back, Charly." Thomas rubbed the scruff on his cheeks and rocked forward in the chair.

"Who's back, Thomas?" Charly knew who he was talking about, she just hoped she'd heard him wrong.

"Alex! Who else would I be talking about?" Thomas let out a laugh that was borderline manic and chills went up Charly's back.

Charly couldn't look at Thomas. She stared out at the road in front of her house. "Thomas, Alex is gone." She gripped her chair like she would fall out of it if she didn't hold on. "I think you should see someone."

Thomas turned towards Charly. His eyes looked feverish and lost, making Charly want to hug him. She was about to when he burst out laughing. It was a hysterical laugh, one that sounded overly jovial and desperate. Thomas stopped laughing as quickly as he started.

"Remember when I was trying to learn how to play the guitar?"

Charly nodded.

"Well, Alex bought me this guitar pedal called a Talk Box." He smiled and pinched the bridge of his nose. "Man… It's almost as if she knew what she was doing. Anyway, it's an effects pedal that echoes back what you just played. About three months ago, I decided to pick up the guitar again. I was depressed and wanted to just end everything. The pain of losing her had become too much."

Charly gasped. "Please, Thomas. If you ever feel like that again, promise, you'll come to talk to me."

Thomas smiled and patted Charly's hand. "I'm fine now. I'm great. I get to talk to my wife every week at exactly 1:13 p.m. on Wednesday. She speaks to me through the Talk Box." Thomas said the last part like he was talking about having a conversation with someone at the grocery store.

Charly couldn't remember a time when she had been so worried about someone. She paused and tried to think about her words before she said them. The last thing she wanted him to do was to get mad and leave after what he had just told her.

"Thomas, I…"

"I know you think I'm going crazy. Shit, I did too when it first happened. I thought the damn thing was broken and picking up a radio station. Then I heard Alex's voice." Tears ran down Thomas's cheeks. "I asked her if she was in the meadow, and she said yes. She'd found a way to let me know she was okay. Then she told me she could only talk once a week because it took so much energy. So, she chose the time she died to live again."

"Thomas, I'm worried about you. It is completely normal to have a breakdown."

"I'm not having a breakdown." Thomas's words came out through gritted teeth. Charly had never seen the man this mad about anything. It made her uneasy. She scanned left and right down the street, looking for anyone that might be out. There was no one.

"I'm sorry," he said. "Look, you don't have to believe me now. Next week you can come see. Alex wants to talk to you." Thomas's smile made Charly feel the chills again, but she smiled back. Whatever was happening made him happy, and that's all she wanted for her friend.

"Okay, Thomas, I'll come by next week."

"Come a minute or two early. I start to hear her at exactly 1:13 p.m. sharp." Thomas said it like they were planning a lunch date. Not talking to his dead wife.

He got up and stretched. "I can't wait for you to see." His face beamed with happiness and excitement. He squeezed Charly's shoulder then hopped down her front stairs. Charly watched Thomas cross the street and felt the dread that hung over her like a blanket. She needed to get her friend some help.

Wednesday came slowly. Every day Charly came home from work and stared across the street at Thomas's house. *I'll see how far gone he is and then act accordingly,* Charly thought. *I'll get him the help he needs.*

She loved and trusted Thomas, and she knew in her heart of hearts he'd never do anything to harm her, but her mother hadn't raised a fool. She always taught her to be prepared for anything. Last year, she'd bought a long pocketknife when she had decided she wanted to try whittling. It would have to be protection enough. Just thinking about it made her feel like she was betraying Alex in some way, but she didn't remove it from her back pocket.

It was 1:11 p.m. when she crossed the street. She hadn't seen Thomas leave or come back from anywhere all day. Charly figured he must have stayed home from work. She saw the note on the door before she'd even walked up Thomas's front steps. *Come on in* was written in black marker on a piece of notebook paper, and Charly could see that the door was open slightly like before.

She pushed the door open. The front room was dark once again, but she could see regular light coming from down the hall.

"Charly, hurry up, the Talk Box is almost ready," Thomas said.

She walked to the beginning of the hallway and saw Thomas standing in the doorway of his and Alex's room. He had an excited expression on his face, along with a hint of irritability. "Come on, it's going to start."

"All right, I'm coming, I'm coming," Charly said. Seeing the excitement on Thomas's face made her relax a little.

When she got to the door, she stopped inside of the door frame and looked into the room. Thomas had the Talk Box hooked up to a small amplifier that was putting off an almost silent feedback sound that was getting louder by the second. Thomas's face had changed to something like crazy ecstasy.

"She's coming, Charly!"

Charly heard a pop from the amp then a voice she hadn't heard in almost a year.

"Hello, baby. Did you bring Charly?" the voice from the amp said.

Charly's eyes misted with tears. *He wasn't crazy,* she thought. The voice from the amp sounded exactly like Alex.

"I did. She's here, my love."

"Good."

The voice had changed. It sounded lower and guttural. Not Alex's sweet sing-song voice. As if Charly needed any more proof that this wasn't her friend, a blue mist came out of the amp and formed into a bright blue ball. Charly was mesmerized for a moment, until the mist started to form into a face.

The thing that materialized before her had long stringy hair, dark opal eyes that had no white around them, and a large gaping mouth full of tiny sharp teeth.

"I'm sorry, Charly, my love needed a body. Until now she hasn't had enough energy to come through. You were like a beacon of light for her. Now we can be together again. You understand, don't you?"

Charly's heart galloped in her chest and her guts felt heavy with betrayal. "Thomas, that's not Alex!" She had time to whimper before the thing flung itself at her face. The mist enveloped her nostrils and mouth. Some of the substance even disappeared into her ears. Charly fell to the floor. She scratched at her neck and face for a few seconds then lay perfectly still.

The thing that used to be Charly watched Thomas walk over to it. He looked odd to it. It studied the dark circles under Thomas's eyes and gazed at the muscles in his limbs. It reached the conclusion quickly that this was a human man of moderate strength. If it struck fast, it should be able to extinguish the human's life. The man's big blinking eyes looked down at it and the thing found its soft spot. The thing smiled up at Thomas. It watched as the man's eyes got big. The hope that the thing saw in them almost made it have pity for the poor dumb creature.

"My love? Alex? Are you there?"

The thing that used to be Charly reached behind the hosts back and grabbed the pocketknife from the back pocket of Charly's pants.

That's right, just a bit closer, it thought.

"Alex, my…"

The thing sunk the knife deep into Thomas's eye, all the way to the handle. It felt his bones crunch. One eye stared at it and the thing pushed the knife in farther. It twisted the knife and felt hard things mix with soft gelatinous things.

The thing looked down Charly's arm and into Thomas's one eye and felt nothing. It threw Thomas's lifeless body across the room and stood up.

The Charly thing looked down at the blood on its shirt, then at Thomas lying in the corner.

"Alex? Never heard of him."

Absolute Dark
Paul B. Kohler

I

THEY SAY WHEN YOU die in a dream, you die in actual life. Kind of like if you were to jump off a skyscraper and plummet to your death, you'd never reach pavement. And if you did, it'd be lights out.

Who are *they* to know this? If they personally experienced death in a dream, in theory, they would have also experienced it in actual life. Therefore, how would anyone know that they were dreaming about dying if they were no longer living to share the experience?

Or, did they experience someone else's death in their own dream, therefore extrapolating the cause of death while dreaming about someone else?

More dream research is needed to determine if one's own mortality is in jeopardy within the depths of their own sleep patterns.

II

When we lived on Earth, free time was usually spent outside, in nature; either hiking or on family picnics. Here on Vobos-3 life is much different.

I was between shifts working on the terraforming rig and was spending time with my daughter. Actually, I was hanging out in our hab, alone, and my daughter was up in her bunk—surfing Skynet, no doubt. And I know what most would say, but it's true, they actually do allow families on deep space missions, especially when terraforming new planets is the objective. Otherwise, the workers would go insane—much like my wife, Hannah, did more than two years ago. But I digress.

Like I said, I was on a bit of downtime and catching up on the news from home—news from Earth. I was relaxing on the gravity couch; an incredible device the scientists back home created to replicate the Earth's gravity here on Vobos. The gravity here is substantially less than that of Earth, and it's quite overwhelming because of its general lack of planetary motion.

Anyway, I was lying there in our hab ... and let me tell you, these units are like no other. They're not just tin cans scattered about the alien world. No, not at all. They tried to mimic our earthly surroundings as much as possible. You know, creature comforts from home.

For example, our hab has a living room, a kitchen, and a small dining area, all clustered on the main level. Up the steep ship ladder, there are two bedrooms and a bathroom. I know it sounds luxurious, but there's nothing grandiose about it. The spaces are really quite ... economical in their use of floor space.

So, there I was, lying on the grav couch, kiddo was upstairs trying to distance herself from her old man. I was drifting in and out of a catnap while the news was droning on in the background. I occasionally looked out the quadruple pane window at the arid landscape. And although the atmosphere outside was breathable, it wasn't quite up to human standards, yet. To limit our exposure to the environment, we were typically scheduled to work rather short shifts. No more than three hours at a time. It was three hours on and two hours off, to be precise. That cycle repeated three times per day, with 14 hours in between cycles. That was our 29-hour Vobian day.

It had been like that for the last 814 Vobian days, the equivalent of nearly three Earth years. But this day was turning out to be quite different.

Anyway, I was lying there, and I was staring outside, and in the distance the weather was ... stark. No more than usual, to be honest, but there was something about the atmosphere that was peculiar. And when I say all of us wayfarers longed to see a blue sky, I'm not exaggerating one bit. The mustard yellow skies on this planet reminded me so much of baby vomit, it's not even funny. But today, that baby vomit sky was mixed with a nice eddy of milk chocolate swirls. Not only that, the activity was high. I mean, the atmosphere seemed like it was moving faster than commonly possible with our limited gravitational pull.

III

I dropped my feet to the floor and stood up a little too quickly. With our reduced gravity, I nearly vaulted myself to the ceiling. But my eyes never left the impending doom. The darkened cloud mixture was moving at a rapid pace now, and it was heading right toward us.

"Hey, kiddo, you see that out the front window?" I knew she wouldn't hear me right away; she probably had her earphones in. "Marie!"

I leaned my forehead against the glass and watched as several of the other colonists began to take notice of the cloud formation. Strangely, it was as if they were all frozen in their tracks, gawking at a disastrous train wreck rapidly approaching.

"What, dad?" Marie's rebellious tone echoed throughout our unit.

"Look out front. Do it now. Do you see it?"

I didn't wait for an answer.

Seeing as I was in between shifts, I still had my environmental suit on, just having unzipped the top portion. I quickly rezipped it and donned my helmet. I stepped into the vestibule and waited for Marie to catch up. "Are you coming?"

"Holy Hell, dad. What is it?" She nearly tumbled down the steps, but the lack of full gravity saved her from taking a header into the support beam.

"No idea, kiddo. Let's go take a look."

A moment later, Marie was standing by my side, also having jumped into her own enviro-suit. We moved out through the vestibule and into the gloom.

If you've ever stepped from the comfort of your own home and into a virtual tropical storm, you'd understand what it was like. The whirlwind, not two meters from our hab, nearly sucked us up. The other colonists from the surrounding units were all huddled together, trying to maintain some sort of mass grounding. Like that was going to work.

Marie and I joined the nearest cluster and stared up in disbelief. The ever-darkening clouds were lowering the ceiling height in the area. I felt as if I could reach up and touch the clouds. An obvious exaggeration, but the oddity of the situation was surreal.

Then, suddenly, it was like a tornado. A funnel dropped from the cloud and touched the ground. The cyclone began kicking up Vobian dust and debris about 30 meters away from where we were standing. The majority of the colonists around us were wearing their terraforming gear. Still, others like Marie, only had their light-duty enviro-suits on. No helmet, just a slightly thicker jumpsuit than one would typically wear inside their hab. With the debris flying around, my immediate concern was for everyone's safety.

"Marie, go grab your helmet and get the PVD. Do it quick." Thankfully, Marie did not need to be told twice as she ran back to our hab and disappeared through the port door. I returned my gaze toward the cyclone as it continued to bounce across the surface. It never really stayed down, touching the ground for any concernable amount of time. It just skipped along at a moderate pace.

"Jesus," I gasped. I spun around to see if Marie had returned yet, but only found that more of the colonists had left the comforts of their own units and joined the mass assembling outside. "This is not going to be good."

A few moments later, I felt the tug on my sleeve; Marie had returned. She did as I had asked and had donned her own helmet as she handed me the PVD.

PVD is short for Personal Video Device for all you Earthers. Each family grouping in the colonnade received one upon landing. It was part of our welcome kit. I guess they wanted us to document what life was like early on. We were the history makers, reluctant or otherwise. And well, this was something that was going to go down in history, I'm sure.

I took the PVD from Marie and flipped it on. As I started recording, the cyclone moved much closer. I had to zoom out to catch its entirety in one frame. It was moving so quickly that I could barely focus. In that horrifying moment, I noticed something that I was nearly certain none of the other colonists could see with their naked eye. This was no regular weather cyclone.

It was machine-like.

In the briefest of moments, I could see mechanical jaws open and consume a colonist before bouncing back up into the cloud. I gasped.

"Marie, get back to the hab. Do it now. Don't come out until it's gone."

"What is it, dad?" she asked, taking a few steps back. "You're scaring me."

"I don't know, but just get inside. And close the blast shutters once you're in."

Thankfully, she didn't dillydally. She ran with great urgency—more than I'd witnessed from her in a long time—and into our hab. I watched her every step just to make sure she followed my instructions. Being a single parent of a 15-year-old girl, you just never know what you're going to get.

By the time I refocused my sight on the monstrosity, it was nearly upon us. Thankfully, the mass of colonists had begun to disperse. I still had the PVD on, trying to focus as best I could, but the cyclone was moving at a frenzied pace. It just kept popping up into the air and then dropping down like it was dotting the ground. And with each poke, we lost another colonist. Hysteria spread quickly as the other colonists began to recognize what was actually happening: The cyclone was murdering our own population. I kept at it, though, trying to capture what was happening on the PVD.

As I watched in horror, I tried to second guess which direction it was going so I could get even closer. It looked like it was heading away from me and to the right, so I followed a few steps behind, continuing to adjust the zoom. Just as I got it dialed in, the cyclone dipped down, and just like before, a mechanical jaw opened and swallowed up Cliff, my shift supervisor, who I'd just had a meeting with, not two hours earlier. He was no more than five meters from me. And this time, before the jaw retracted into the swirling cyclone, I noticed something else.

There appeared to be some kind of eye on the front edge, just above the metallic mandible. It was quite humanlike as it articulated inside its socket. It was looking for its next victim. As soon as it locked its sight on someone else, the device retracted, and the cyclone moved toward the next casualty. And again, just like before, it dropped out of the cloud and consumed Veronica, Barney's wife, and lead civil engineer.

I'd decided then that I had enough footage of the disaster and began to put some distance between it and myself. I still left the PVD on, but I backstepped as best I could. Obviously, I did not want to stumble and fall. And that's when I saw it. The articulating eye stared right at me.

Jesus, I'm going to be next.

At that point, I turned and fully ran in the opposite direction. I was not going to let it get me. For the briefest moment, I was thankful for the reduced gravity of Vobos. The strain on my joints was far less than running on Earth. I was able to sprint much faster than I ever had before. I flipped the PVD to front mode to record my own face.

"Marie. If I don't make it back, know that I love you. I know since mom died, it's been tough with just you and I. Trust me, we both loved you more than anything in the world." I could barely keep it together as I recorded what may very well have been my last words to her.

I had no idea if I would need them or not, but I wanted to say something. There I was, running for my life from who-knows-what, this mechanical monster on this alien world. It was chasing me, and I could feel it getting closer. As I ran, I noticed the horrifying faces on the colonists that I whizzed by. They knew it was coming, coming for me. And they knew that there wasn't a damn thing that was going to save me. I felt utterly helpless in that moment.

I held the PVD out in front of me, and on the screen, I could see myself still being recorded. In the very short distance behind me, the spinning cloud was closing in. As if in slow motion, the mechanical jaw dropped out of the cyclone and came right for my head.

But, before it could consume me, I thrust the PVD toward the nearest colonist and yelled, "Take this! Get it to Mar—"

Darkness.

IV

"Marie."

Silence.

"Marie, I know you can hear me."

The low hum of the ion engines droned on, but otherwise, nothing but silence.

"Marie! Come sit down this instant," Hannah said as she nervously adjusted her own seat harness. "I can't believe you talked us into this, Scott." Hannah turned her attention to her husband.

Scott was intently studying the specifications of the terraforming reactor that he'd be building on Vobos-3. "Hmm?"

"Are you even listening to me?" Hannah waved her hand in front of his face, drawing his attention toward her.

"Oh, Hannah," Scott moaned. "I don't think you can lay this on me. It was your idea from the start. Besides, it's for the greater good. You know as well as I that without this outpost, Earth stands no chance against the Dominion. We made this decision as a family, including the heavy hand of your mother. If your dad had his way, we'd obviously be home right now, barbequing up some exotic meat he'd trapped in the wild."

Hannah's eyes narrowed as Marie finally floated into the seat next to her. "Thank you, sweetheart. Would you please fasten your safety harness? Commander Brooks will no doubt be by to check in on us."

Marie fumbled with the six-point harness as she fought to hold herself from floating away again. Zero-g's had its challenges. She giggled.

"Remember how I showed you, kiddo," Scott said as he demonstrated for what must've been the 10th time on their journey. "First, you hold the center buckle over your chest. Next, you take the middle strap on your right-hand side and fasten it in. Then, counterclockwise around your belly, fasten each and every one until you've made a full circle. The first two straps will hold you in place while you finish everything off."

Marie nearly rose to the ceiling before Hannah grabbed her leg and pulled her back down to the cushion of the seat. Once down, she followed her father's instructions and, one by one, attached each of the harness straps to the center clutch. Upon finishing, Marie looked up and smiled.

"Great job, kiddo." Scott winked and gave her a thumbs up.

"And there's that, too," Hannah continued. "All you want to do is be her best friend. Can't you be her father once in a while?"

"Jesus, Hannah. She's twelve years old. You don't have to overreact at every single thing that happens." Scott returned to his technical manual, barely able to focus on what was in front of him.

After some time, he closed the book and looked around the cabin. Across the aisle, Todd McBride, Scott's superior and lifelong friend, sat next to his wife, Darla. They were both fast asleep. In front of them and to the left sat another couple that Scott remembered seeing on the manifest but didn't know them personally. They were also asleep.

Once he was sure they would not be overheard, he spoke. "Hey, hon, you remember what the doctor said?" Scott chose his words carefully.

"I do. Your point?"

"Oh, Hannah. Even he agreed that it was probably a good thing for you, mentally, to get off Earth. A change of scenery was going to do you better than the medication that you've been taking. Isn't that worth something?"

Scott glanced over at Marie; she too was dozing off. Scott remembered that, as they approached the jump gate, the oxygen level in the cabin was going to thin slightly and, in turn, would cause drowsiness. He felt the pull of sleep inside his head.

Hannah sighed heavily. "I ... I know. It's just so—" She paused and rubbed her temples gently. "It's just so fast. It seems like we just talked about going on this six-month mission, yesterday."

"You know it wasn't yesterday, Hannah. It was nearly a year ago when we signed up for this."

"But did we have to sell everything? I mean, couldn't we have put things in storage for when we return? We are returning, right?"

It was Scott's turn to sigh. "Yes, dear. We're going to return. But what if we like this ... this new life? What if being colonists on a new world is really what we're good at? It seems like nonsense to continue paying some kind of storage credit indefinitely, while we, I don't know, skip around the universe until we find where we really want to call home. It's just better this way."

"Is *that* what this is all about? Really?" Scott asked, fighting the urge to fall asleep. "Is it that all our possessions—"

Just then, the forward gangway hatch opened and in stepped Commander Brooks. Once inside, he closed the hatch just as abruptly. Scott paused their conversation for a moment as he analyzed Brooks' demeanor.

Commander Jason Brooks was a hard-nosed military man that Scott had dealings with in the past. He was not a man to cross, and he spoke truthfully. He was no-nonsense, and that was needed for this mission.

"Folks, we're approaching the jump gate. It's probably best that you all get some shut-eye. I know this is your first time going through, and it's not as pleasant of an experience as one might think. There's nothing to see out the port windows, and the entire experience leaves you quite queasy. Experience dictates that the exposure is far less invading when you're asleep. But again, the choice is yours how you want to experience it."

The commander spoke the words as he walked through the passenger cabin, glancing at each of the passengers—the future colonists of Vobos-3.

"How long will we be in the jump gate, commander?" Scott asked as Brooks walked by.

"From the point of entry here in this sector to the moment we come out in the Malfinio Expanse, it'll be about 90 minutes."

"That's it?" Hannah asked. "I thought our journey was going to take months."

"Cumulatively, yes. It is a four-month itinerary. Once we're out of the jump gate, we still have a few month's cruising time left." The commander appeared agitated at Hannah's questioning. "All of this should have been explained before we left. Did nobody talk to you?"

Hannah guffawed. "Oh, yes. I remember now. I'm sorry, commander. I'm just a little *off*, I guess. We'll be sure to get some shut-eye, as you suggest."

Commander Brooks nodded and continued his path through the cabin and out through the rear hatchway. As soon as the hasps were engaged, Scott spoke up.

"Hannah, have you already stopped taking your medication?"

Hannah ignored Scott's question. She eased her seat back, closed her eyes, and very nonchalantly brushed her chest against Scott's resting arm. "We must get some sleep, Scott. Commander's orders."

Scott chuckled and rested his hand on Hannah's thigh. "You really are too much sometimes, dear. Maybe that's why I love you so."

Hannah placed her hand on top of Scott's then leaned into him as they both drifted off to sleep.

The passenger cabins lights dimmed until all that was left was pure darkness.

V

Darkness.

I could say no more words before I was entirely consumed by the monstrosity's mammoth jaws. I did a quick check of my facilities and was surprised to find that I was in no pain. It appeared that none of my limbs were broken, or severed, for that matter.

As I tried to balance myself in my new alien surroundings, I was thrown hard against a metal surface. "So much for no broken bones," I mumbled as I heard a gruesome snap in my ribcage. And then came the pain. Without even a moment to catch my breath, I began tumbling in all directions, unsure which way was up. I tried to stabilize myself by thrusting my arms out to my sides until I made contact with what felt like curved walls. I tried to grasp a hold of something, but my hands came up empty. With no way of seeing, it felt as if I were encased in a large clothes dryer from back on Earth. Then it hit me. Or, was it that I hit the side with my helmet?

My helmet!

I reached up and turned the mounted headlight on. It flickered at first but then shone brightly. I found that I was in a circular steel shaft. Along one edge, there were metal bars, almost like rungs of a ladder. I wasn't sure how, but I somehow avoided grasping any one of them as I was spinning out of control. I was sure, however, that one of them was the culprit for my newly sustained injury, and I was shocked that I hadn't end up impaled on one of them. Not exactly being a God-fearing man, I moved on without gratitude and started climbing in what I thought was the up direction.

As I ascended, it was nearly impossible to keep myself from losing my grip, both figuratively and literally. The fresh pain in my chest did me no favors, either. The more I was jostled around, the more I was sure at least two or three of my ribs were broken.

After several dozen steps, I noticed that the rungs were coated in some kind of wetness. Upon closer inspection, it appeared to be blood, probably human. I stopped for a moment and looked back down. I could see flashes of daylight as the mechanical jaw again started up its motion, opening, and closing. It was hunting for its next victim. I looked ahead of me, or above me as it was, to see if I could find another person—it's previous victim—but nobody was in sight.

"Think." *What can I do?*

I was still wearing my terraforming suit when it hit me. "Wait, do I still have it?"

I fumbled through my pockets, and sure enough, I found a handful of detonators that I had been using earlier in the day.

"Jackpot."

By then, I had noticed the daylight from below had stopped its intermittent flashing. I was still being jostled around, but it appeared that either something was blocking the light from reaching me or the monstrosity had stopped feeding.

"Hello!" I yelled.

My voice merely echoed around me. The curved steel seemed to somehow deaden my tone. I tried again.

"Is anybody there!"

All I could hear was the whirring sound of the monstrosity, and a little bit of my own heartbeat pounding inside my chest.

Then, I heard it. It was faint at first, but as the seconds ticked by, I was sure what it was.

"S-Scott? Is that you?"

"Holy shit!" She's still alive.

VI

"Scott, is that you?" The voice was screaming now, and Scott could barely make out where it was coming from.

"Hannah, where are you? I can't find you." Scott continued climbing the metal stairway in near darkness. Having been assigned to the subterranean excavation division, being this high up in the reactor core was somewhat out of his comfort level. He didn't know what anything really was or where each of the blind corridors or stairways led to.

"I'm here. But be careful, the monsters are everywhere!"

What was she talking about? Scott wondered. He knew it was a bad idea to completely take her off her medication, but that argument was in the past.

As he reached the top of the stairway, he was faced with two decisions. First, step outside the conical structure and into the alien atmosphere. That wasn't an option. Second, he could walk across a narrow platform into the peak of the reactor core. "Jesus Christ. I'm not a fan of that option, either."

But Hannah's latest scream drove him forward without hesitation. He stepped out onto the steel gangway, his hands gripping tightly to the side rails as he inched himself out into the open air of the reactor. After several steps, he finally caught sight of Hannah. She was standing near the end of the platform, her back toward him.

"My God, Hannah! Get back from there! There's no railing in front of you, you could fall." Scott increased his pace but did not want to startle Hannah.

"I-I can't. I can't … make it stop! Scott, they're everywhere. Can't you see?"

"Slow down, Hannah," Scott begged. "What are you talking about? It's just you and I here."

Hannah's eyes enlarged far bigger than Scott had ever witnessed, and darted all around, not stopping to focus on any one thing.

"They're everywhere!" She hissed and then let out another gut-wrenching scream.

"Hush, hush baby," he said, hoping to soothe her. He tried to remember what the doctor back on Earth had told them about how to cope with her hallucinations if they were to come back. But in this situation, Scott only drew a blank. His mind was utterly overloaded by his surroundings. He stepped forward. "Honey, it's going to be okay. I won't let them get—"

"Don't patronize me!" she yelled. "You're just like everyone else. Why is it I'm the only one that can see these … these aliens? These alien monsters! They're everywhere." Hannah leaned out over the edge of the platform and looked straight down. From their height, Scott assumed that they were close to three-hundred meters above the floor surface below.

Having inched that much closer to Hannah, he could see the sweat covering her skin. And her hand, moist as it was, was barely holding on to the steel handrail. He knew that she could let go at any moment.

Scott took another cautious step forward, now only about two meters from Hannah. "Baby, I believe you. I can see them everywhere too. Just step back, and we can talk about how to make them go away." Scott prayed that his tactic would not backfire. Of course, he couldn't see the alien monsters that she'd been rambling on about for the better part of a month. He'd just chalked it up as playful banter because every time Hannah brought it up, she would giggle and laugh it off. He prayed to God that he could've seen the signs sooner.

"Y-you do? You see them? Do you see…" Hannah paused and turned to face Scott. She gazed passed him and onto the platform beyond. "Do, do you see that one right there, Scott? Tell me you see it."

Scott turned, looked, but there was nothing there. He took a deep breath and began to nod his head.

"Oh, that's not that scary. I see it, and it's—"

"You sonofabitch. You don't see it! All you can do is patronize me. You think that my medication levels are way off, I can read right through you, you bastard."

Before Scott could stop her, Hannah turned and stepped right up to the edge of the platform and was about to step off.

"Wait! Don't do it," Scott pleaded as he lunged for Hanna's arm.

Hannah fully stepped off the platform and began falling, but before her momentum took over, Scott grabbed her wrist as he fell to the platform surface.

The look on Hannah's face was of profound confusion. Then as the seconds ticked by, her eyes grew wide with terror. Full, unbridled terror.

"S-Scott! Get me up! Help me!"

Scott felt Hanna's sweat between his hand and her wrist, and he was beginning to lose his grip. "Baby, give me your other hand. Reach up, grab my—"

Before Hannah could react, her damp wrist slipped from Scott's hand, and she plummeted to her death.

"Scoooottt!"

VII

"Scott? That you?" Came a distant voice from below.

"Oh, Hannah!" I yelled.

"Uh, no, sir. You bump your head or somethin'? It's me, Mags."

My God, it got Maggie!

Maggie was an early colonist that refused to return to Earth after her last tour. She said that she loved the place and wouldn't return because this was her new home. And now Maggie was going to die.

"What the hell is going on?" she bellowed. I couldn't see her, but I could hear the fear in her voice.

"Hell if I know, Mags. Are you protected?"

I knew before the question was asked that she'd been decommissioned weeks ago, and that meant she was no longer wearing a company-sponsored environmental suit. But I hoped anyway.

"Um, no. I-I'm just wearing first clothes. Can you believe it?"

Jesus, first clothes were garments given to new colonists upon arrival to wear around our hab units until more suitable attire could be manufactured or provided. They were quite minimalistic and were not made to last for much longer than a few months. But some of us, including myself, and Maggie apparently, still wore them from time to time.

"Quick, climb up to me," I said. "I know it's difficult to see but feel around and you'll find a ladder along one of the sidewalls."

After a few moments, I started to hear the clanking of feet climbing the rungs. The sound echoed flatly through the tube. She was on her way, and as she came closer, my mind raced for a solution. I was holding on to the ladder rung with one hand, and in my other, I was holding one of the blasting caps. All the while, the metal tube we were in continued to shift and spin.

I had a flash. If I could just ignite one of the blasting caps, perhaps it could sever the tube from whatever this monstrosity was.

"Maggie! Are you close?"

"Yeah, I can see your light now. I'm almost there."

"Mags, no. Stay there and hold on to the ladder. I'm going to try something."

I removed the protective cover from the blasting cap and chucked it as far as I could above me. I heard it clank against the sidewall and waited.

And waited.

The 10-second timer seemed to take forever, and I wished I would've changed it to five before throwing it.

And I waited.

Four, three, two … One.

Nothing.

Suddenly, something was pulling on my leg. I looked down, and there was Maggie.

"Jesus, you scared the crap out of me."

"You tried a blasting cap, didn't you?" she asked.

"Yeah, but something happened. I threw it up there, but it didn't go off."

Maggie was old-school. She had more knowledge about terraforming better than anyone I knew. I could only imagine what was going through her head at that very moment. She was probably devising a way for everything to happen just the way it should. She had an engineer's mind for sure.

"Maybe when you threw it, it bounced and switched off. Maybe if you set it and get away?"

"Not enough time. These new caps have a ten-second timer, and that's not near enough time to climb back down."

Just then, from far above, we heard the scream of what most likely was a previous victim.

"What the hell are we going to do, Mags?"

Maggie didn't say anything, but I felt her move up next to me. "Sorry, my friend. I know it's close quarters in here."

She continued to slide her body past and then above me. "I'm just trying to get by."

"Maggie, no. You don't know what it's going to do to you. That scream didn't sound good."

"Quick, hand me another one of your blasting caps."

I fished out another cap and handed it to her. "Maggie? What are you going to do?"

"I'm not sure what the hell this thing is, but I know I'm not going down without a fight. You have a daughter, Scott. I am alone. I'm an old woman living on an alien world, and I have nothing to lose. I'm going to take this blasting cap and shove it up its ass."

"Jesus, no, Maggie. We can figure this out."

From above, another scream.

"Not this time, Scott. Work your way back to the jaw and wait for the explosion. If everything goes right, I'll have severed this part of the monster and hopefully killed whatever is doing this."

Before I could protest, Maggie had already scampered out of sight. She was now in full darkness, and I wish I would've given her my helmet for at least sighting purposes.

As I climbed my way back down toward the metallic mandible, what appeared to be a trapdoor closed right below me. It was as if they knew what was going to happen. I looked up but could only see darkness. If I went back up, I'd risk injury from the explosion. I had to sit.

And wait.

VIII

"Thank you for waiting, Mr. Phillips. Commander McBride is just finishing up a telecall back to Earth. He should be done any moment," McBride's personal assistant Gary said as he tapped away at his communication display.

Scott remained seated at one of the dozen or so gravity chairs scattered around the cavernous administrative unit. Admin was one of the first to be established on Vobos-3, nearly 12 years previous. In comparison, it's quite similar to the colonists' habitation units but at a much grander scale.

Inside the main level resides all engineering disciplines, as well as reactor implementation. There was little doubt that the admin unit would be repurposed as a command center for the impending war against the Dominion. With all the digital displays already plastered upon nearly every surface, it would have been very ideal.

Various solar systems and orbital trajectories were laid out on half of the panels, while the others were detailing specifications of ongoing Vobos-3 projects. And although Scott had been in the admin unit numerous times, never was it for official business-like today. Besides Gary and himself, the room was empty, which Scott felt peculiar.

Then, without notice, a tall digital panel just to the right of where Scott sat slid horizontally and disappeared into a wall cavity. Behind it was another room that Scott never knew existed. He sat up and tried to peer in, but before he could catch a glimpse of anything, Commander Todd McBride walked through, and the door closed promptly.

"Hey, Scott. Glad you could make it. How are, um, have you been holding up?" McBride walked up to Scott and shook his outstretched hand. Scott and McBride went way back, all the way back to their college days. Despite the passing years, Scott still looked up to McBride as a superior, even a role model of sorts.

"I suppose I'm doing well, considering. Marie is your typical teenage girl. Her rebellious streak is just starting to form, and that's of concern." Both Scott and McBride chuckled.

"So, Scott. Have you considered my offer? I know it's only been a few weeks since ... the ordeal, but our window is closing."

Scott began to pace around, attempting to analyze the nearest digital display. He did, in fact, make a decision, and it was one that he wasn't proud of. One of the last conversations that he had on Earth was with Hannah's parents, and he remembered the moment vividly. They'd made him promise to protect Hannah while off Earth. And he was damn scared to face them after what had happened.

"Scott?" McBride prodded.

"Yeah, about that. I think Marie and I are fine to stay on Vobos for another tour, if that's all right with you."

McBride stepped up next to Scott, staring at the same display and exhaled. "Scott, if that's what you want, I'll support it. But most everyone here, as well as those back on Earth think it's probably better for you and Marie to return. To head home. If you two don't leave within the next few days, you'll miss the window through the jump gate. You'll be fixed here for at least another eight months. Nothing can change that timeline."

Scott was well aware of the jump window as he'd gone through this process of decision-making numerous times before Hannah died.

"I think I'm okay with that," Scott said, turning to face McBride. "I just feel that I'm not through here, and if you could cut me a little slack, I'll be back up to speed in no time."

McBride's eyes widened, and a slight grin crept across his face. "On a selfish note, I'm happy to hear that, Scott. We have a long history, and I feel that I can guide you through whatever it is that you're dealing with. Quite honestly, it's Marie that I'm concerned ab—"

"Well, she's fine." Scott cut him short.

"Sure, she might be fine now, but what about when she starts really missing her mom, or distant family for that matter? At least back on Earth—"

"I get it, Todd. But we've talked about it, and our decision is set. We're staying. Talk to me again in eight months, and we'll see if our mood has changed."

McBride slapped Scott on his shoulder then pulled him in for a hug. "I'm here for you, man. Not just as your station commander but, you know, for whatever you need."

Scott returned the embrace and contemplated telling McBride how his dreams, or nightmares rather, have kept him up most nights since it happened. But he didn't want to give his friend any more reason to force him home. He'd just have to live with the screams in his mind.

Scott broke from the hug before it got awkward. "Thanks."

"Don't mention it. Really, we're understaffed as it is, and having you around for at least another cycle certainly relieves the pressure from back home. How about you take the next couple of weeks and just ease your way back into things. I won't expect anything monumental from you until you tell me you're ready. Deal?"

"Sounds good, Todd."

IX

After waiting a bit, I decided to be somewhat proactive about the situation. I'd noticed the cyclone monstrosity had started slowing its gyration. Seeing as I was not being knocked around like a ragdoll anymore, I switched my focus to the trapdoor below. Unless I could get it open, the odds of me surviving the ordeal were not significant.

I took an inventory of what I had in my environmental suit's pockets: I still had three more blasting caps, a sparging wrench, and half a dozen wire leads. I examined the trapdoor, but it was void of any fasteners. It was a smooth sheet-metal like substance that spanned from one side to the other of the cylindrical tube.

My first effort was to try and kick through. I gripped the lowest ladder rung and lifted myself up as far as my arms would allow. Then, I dropped as fast and hard as possible onto the trapdoor. I felt a small budge but not enough to make a difference. I tried this a few more times with the same result. Then I got the idea to possibly drive my wrench into the edge where the trapdoor met the sidewall. Amazingly enough, I was able to get the wrench's tip down into the crack a few centimeters, until I heard the next scream.

I froze and stared up. Obviously, it came from Maggie. *My God. It's too late.*

Abruptly, her screams stopped and were replaced with actual words. But they were spoken so far away I could barely make out what she was saying.

"Garble, garble *hold* garble *something* garble," and then it broke off. It was dead silent for the next thirty-seconds and then another horrendous scream.

"AHHHH!"

In mid-scream, the monstrosity began to move quite differently than it had up until then. The twisting and shaking that my aching body became accustomed to were replaced by a low rumble that practically vibrated the molars out of my mouth. Just as I thought the vibrations had reached their peak, they got worse. Far worse. I dropped my tools and placed my hands over my ears because the sound was so loud. Then, the vibrations just stopped.

Hesitantly, I pulled my hands from my ears and waited for a second or two before dropping my hands to my side.

That was one of those moments that I wished I wouldn't've reacted so quickly. The explosion that came was so earsplittingly loud, I could feel my ears begin to bleed. Literally. And then, just as suddenly, the entire monstrosity began revolting and spinning and shaking in all directions. Unfortunately, I could not grasp hold of anything to stabilize myself. I just had to ride it out.

At one point, the upward force drove me down onto the trapdoor so hard that I felt it begin to buckle. As I laid there, pinned to the metal plate, my darkness was interrupted when far above, shards of light began to creep into the metallic cylinder. At first, the light was faint, but it was there. Then, moment by moment, I could see the seams of the cylinder begin to split. It started from way up high and worked its way down toward where I was. After a while, I felt the pressure relieve a bit, and I was able to right myself and stand up. Just as I did so, the splitting metal tore all the way around and launched me out into the sky.

"Sonofabitch!"

It only took a moment for me to realize why I was feeling so much pressure on that trapdoor. It was because of the force caused by the monstrosity jutting up into the sky. I was now falling to the Vobian surface, nearly 500 meters below, if I had to guess.

As I plummeted, I could feel my heart beating, pounding ever harder. The wetness leaking from my ears spread across my face as the wind whipped by.

"Oh, Hannah. Baby, I'm coming to you," I declared, suddenly realizing the eerie similarities between her death and my own impending doom.

As I tried to maintain focus, my vision began to cloud over. I was going to lose consciousness, thankfully, before impacting onto the surface of Vobos-3.

"I love you, Marie. I wish—I wish I were a better father."

I repeated these words over and over, willing them into her mind. It was the only thing I could do to maintain any sense of awareness.

As I fell toward the rapidly approaching surface, I sensed more and more of my vision escape me. It was minor at first, but then it became so enveloping, all I could see was black.

At the moment just before impact, I was surrounded by absolute dark, and only silence could be heard.

X

At the moment of impact, I opened my eyes and stared up at the ceiling. I expected to see the mixture of baby vomit clouds but instead found Marie's face hovering over me.

"Dad? Dad, are you all right?" Marie said as she shook me.

"Wha, what happened?"

"You fell off the grav couch, again."

"Again?" I sat up and patted my chest out of instinct. The anticipated rib pain was nonexistent. "Again?"

Marie rolled her eyes. "I thought you'd gone back to work, and I came down to fix a snack. I found you thrashing around on the floor. Dad, you really scared me. Are you all right?"

I stood, rushed to the window, and stared out. "I, I must've been just having a bad dream or something." I rubbed the sleep from my eyes and turned toward Marie. "Has there been any weather changes today?"

Marie stepped up to the window and peered out. "Like what? It's been like this for, I don't know, since we got here all those years ago. It's just so ... drab."

"Tell me about it, kiddo." I chuckled. "Do you think we've overstayed our welcome? You think it's time for us to go home? Go back to Earth?"

I watched her and waited for a reaction. At first, there was nothing. But then it appeared that blood drained from her face. She backed up and sat down on the edge of the gravity couch.

"Dad, are you being serious right now?" Her eyes wide.

I sat down next to her, and she leaned her head on my shoulder. "I don't know, kiddo, but I think we might have gotten just about all we can from this place. With everything that we've gone through here, it might be time for us to move on."

We sat in silence for several minutes, neither one of us knowing quite what to say. As we sat there, my mind replayed various snippets of my dream. What did it mean? What did any of it mean?

Finally, I took a deep breath and asked, "Are you ready to hear about it?"

She didn't answer right away, but I could feel her tears begin to fall on my arm.

Her head nodded almost imperceptibly. "Yes. I think so."

I wrapped my arms around her and held her tight. "I was with your mom when she died. Here's what happened."

The End... Again

Jessica West

KIRSTEN COULD FEEL THE flesh in her most tender place tearing as the baby's head crowned. It took all of her strength and will to hold in the screams trying to claw their way out of her chest. If they found her here, her baby would be dead within minutes of its birth.

Kirsten's death would come soon either way.

While the contraction was at its peak, she pushed. Her legs trembled with the effort, but it wasn't enough to expel the baby. For one horrific moment, she imagined the umbilical cord as some sort of monstrous tentacle wrapping itself around her baby and dragging its little body back inside her. Almost as if she'd made it happen by thinking such thoughts, the contraction faded and the painful pressure and tearing eased.

She wept. Not from fear or pain or even relief. She wept at her own stupidity. Her baby would not die. Certainly not from any monster. The night of its conception, He promised her this baby would defeat the monster horde running rampant across the planet. They would not find her here. She would fulfill her end of the bargain and bring a saviour into this world alive.

Kirsten gasped at the onset of another contraction, took a deep breath, and pushed for all she was worth.

Lilith turned at the corner of Second and Holly Streets, and walked across the deserted parking lot of one of the few grocery stores that still had power. The generator sounded like a train. Surprisingly, there were no zombies. Maybe the only sounds that drew them were screams and such. Either way, a grocery store was probably a good idea.

"Smart girl," she muttered to herself. The surrogate had no doubt hidden herself away in the cooler. Good for keeping the smell from reaching the mindless, ravenous horde.

"No good for our baby boy, though." He would need warmth. Even an exceptional lad like himself would need a moment to acclimate to this new existence.

"I hope I'm not too late." She shifted into wolf form and scented the air. The unmistakable stench of blood and rotting flesh burned her nostrils.

Lilith growled low, deep in her throat. *That better not be His blood.*

Damien opened his eyes and shuddered. The world was a blur of shapes against a bright light, all encapsulated in a cold atmosphere. A flash of memory, from his father's days in the frozen lake of the Ninth Circle of Hell, jarred his mind at the same moment a pair of hands lifted him.

His arms flailed out at his sides of their own accord. He made his tiny hands into tight fists, gaining control of his limbs quickly but not quickly enough for his liking.

The pair of hands drew him closer to a face, all of which likely belonged to the surrogate. If she survived long enough for him to speak, he would thank her. Father was a stickler for manners.

The surrogate unbuttoned her flannel shirt and tucked him inside, wrapping him first with one side of the shirt then the other. She guided his mouth to her breast.

He didn't need the guidance, but it sometimes helped the surrogates to let them believe he was totally helpless. Until he fed, he was close enough to helpless. He was killable, anyway. The world didn't have time for him to die and repeat this whole grueling process. This time, humanity had taken their idiocy too far.

As he suckled, Damien sent out waves of soothing energy to the exhausted surrogate, hoping to lull her into sleep before truly feeding. Most of his surrogates died in their sleep. It was the humane way of doing this, and part of the agreement his Father had made with the human Father.

The surrogate drifted off, and Damien extended his tiny fangs into one of the large blue veins running across the top of her breast. As he drank deeply, a lifetime of her experiences—including knowledge of the zombie apocalypse currently threatening humanity—flooded his mind.

Her arms weakened as her pulse slowed and died. If it hadn't been for the shirt she'd so snugly wrapped him in, he'd have rolled right down her torso.

Damien took the opportunity to flex the muscles in his arms, legs, and back as much as he could. The scent of decay drifted to him. His keen senses could detect it despite the cold air. The distance was uncertain, though.

He could wait for them to find him here, and risk the mindless creatures not making it this far, or venture out of this cooler to meet them head-on. He'd have to open the door and desecrate the surrogate's corpse to lure the zombies to him. Damien was loathe to destroy the woman who brought him into the world. So he decided on a compromise between the two options.

He'd wait until they were closer, then he'd attack. In the meantime, he'd thank his surrogate by snuggling in close and napping in her arms.

Sudden silence and complete darkness woke Damien several hours later. His surrogate's arms, fallen to her sides as he slept, had gone cold and hard. The room itself still held a chill which caressed the exposed flesh of his left side from his shoulder down to his toes. The floor beneath his feet was frigid. The top of his head resting under her chin, and the right side of his body nestled against hers, were warm despite the coolness of her flesh.

Damien stood slowly, testing his newly grown muscles and bones.

The nauseating smell of rot threatened to overwhelm him. They were close. It seemed as though the mindless undead had found him after all.

He stretched and flexed, warming up for the fight to come.

Moans and guttural growls issued from outside the cooler. The sound of the generator had probably drawn them this close, but they'd never think to open a door and search in here.

Damien's eyes adjusted to the darkness. He opened the door slowly and quietly, but the horde jerked in his direction as if he'd fired a gun.

The isles were thick with them. Everywhere he looked, a line of zombies three and four wide filled the spaces between the row of coolers where he was born and the world of humans he was to save outside.

It always happened like this. The surrogate was supposed to buy him as much time as possible. He never grew past twenty years old. This time, judging by his height, it looked like he'd only made it to his early teens.

Lilith probably wouldn't make it in time to save him this time either.

With a deep sigh, Damien drew forth every ounce of demonic power his still growing body could muster. His teeth and nails elongated, as did his bones. A fierce roar burst from his lungs as pure dark energy filled his muscles. Power surged through his veins.

The horde sprang into action, pouring forth from the isles.

Damien sprinted to the nearest corner, to his left, slashing with his claws at any of the monstrosities that got close enough. If he could keep his back to this corner, maybe he could fight them off long enough for Lilith to arrive. Maybe he would survive this time. He had saved humanity enough times to have earned the right to live, right?

Hurry, Mother.

Tears streamed over Lilith's furry face as she sprinted toward the suddenly quiet and dark grocery store. *Please don't let me be too late.* She swore the last time that she would find a way to die with him if she failed to save him again. Demon or no, she could not keep watching her son die.

Mid-sprint, she shifted back into her human form, drawing forth all of her considerable demonic power and filling her heart with hungry rage. Lilith was moving far too fast to stop for the frozen automatic doors. She burst through the plate glass with nothing more than a low grunt.

Zombies took up every square inch of the store. For one horrible second, she thought maybe the surrogate hadn't hidden in the cooler after all. Maybe that was a dumb assumption on Lilith's part. Her precious Damien may already be dead. She missed a step and stumbled, sliding noisily across the polished floor and right into the backs of the mass of undead.

Lilith kicked and slashed as mindlessly as these creatures, fueled by intense hatred of all the things that had killed her beloved son every time humanity nearly wiped themselves out. She hated the humans most of all. If it weren't for them, none of this would be happening.

But then, if not for them, Damien never would have been born.

One of the undead bit a chunk of flesh out of her shoulder.

She shoved a clawed hand into his stomach and grabbed his intestines, ripping them out and flinging them as far behind her as she could. It wouldn't buy her much time, but the zombies closest to her would take the bait and give her a bit of breathing room. She snapped the neck of the disemboweled zombie and took a rapid survey of the scene before her.

Anger would only get her so far. She needed to focus. They couldn't kill her. Not forever. Not any more than they could kill Damien. Not permanently. But she could still die and repeat the cycle of rebirth. And so could he, again. And that, she could not bear.

Focus.

Lilith pinched her pointer fingers and thumbs together, then drew her hands apart. Between them, shimmering like a spider's web, was a line of dark energy.

This she flung out toward the crowd. The line severed all of the zombies within six feet of her, if the big red stickers at her feet were accurate. Some were decapitated. Some were chopped in two at chest-height. But all of them were dead for true now, their spines severed.

Unfortunately, the line was only about three feet wide. Zombies still surrounded her to her left and right.

She curled her hands and gathered balls of dark energy. With her left hand, she threw one flickering ball of what looked like black flame at the crowd to her left.

The crowd to her right jumped on her before she could unleash the ball in her right hand. She released her grip on it and let the energy find its own target as they fell on top of her, crushing her to the cold floor at her back. It would only take out one zombie, but she would kill as many as she could with her teeth if she had to before she succumbed to death.

She couldn't decide if it was worse to die before seeing him again or watching him die. Both were the kinds of pain a mother should never endure.

Damien hurled himself at the dog pile in the front of the store. *It can't end like this.* All these times she'd arrived too late to save him, only to either find his corpse or hold him as he died, all these times... This time, he made it in time to save him.

But could he save her?

He flung rotting corpses off of her, praying she was still alive. The irony of a demon—the Antichrist himself, no less—praying was not lost on him. But prayer was not reserved solely for humans. Nor was irony.

The corpses he threw against the walls burst like overripe fruit. One particularly vicious corpse lunged at his throat. He pulled back in time and swung his arm, intending to take its head off with one powerful blow. But the creature ducked back at the last second, then lunged again. The creature's teeth sank deep into his arm.

Her nostrils flared and she blinked in surprise, opening her mouth and releasing him.

He raised his arm, fully prepared to smash her head into the floor at her back.

"Damien?"

The son of Lucifer froze for a solid minute, inspecting every inch of her he could see. Aside from a huge chunk of flesh missing from her shoulder, all of her other injuries looked minor. That shoulder would heal quickly enough. She was covered in blood and gore, but he sensed no fatal wounds.

Neither of them had any life threatening injuries.

She gave him as thorough an inspection as he'd given her.

Damien helped her to her feet, and together they finished off the last of the horde threatening humanity this time.

They left the grocery store together without a word. Words would come later. For now, it was enough that they had both survived.

The Lost Tapes: Arrow Lake
Daniel Arthur Smith

"RECORDING BEGINS WITH TODAY'S date, March 24th, 2021. My name is Agent Melissa Muldoon. Present with me is Agent Lawrence Meyer. Commencing interview of Nathaniel Westerhausen regarding the disappearance of Hal Landon and his youngest son Peter Landon, neighbors of Mr. Westerhausen on Arrow Lake. Mr. Westerhausen, we were notified about the disappearance by the local police and we're here today at their invitation. I want to make it clear that we're here to listen and to help. I realize that this can be overwhelming, so if at any time you need a break, or anything at all, just say so."

"I appreciate that."

"Could you please state your name for the record?"

"It's Nathaniel Westerhausen. Everyone calls me Nate, though."

"Thank you, Mr. Westerhausen."

"You don't want to call me Nate?"

"Would it make you feel more comfortable?"

"I think it'll make us both feel more comfortable. I'm eighty-eight, Westerhausen has a lot of syllables, and I don't have that kind of time to waste. We'll be here all day."

"Okay. Nate. As I mentioned we're here with you today because the local police invited us to join the investigation. The reason we're interviewing you is because your selectman, Angus McConnell, said that you had something to share concerning the disappearance of Hal Landon and his ten-year-old son Peter."

"I do. I don't suppose ole Angus gave you a heads up?"

"A heads up?"

"Told you about…"

"About the creature?"

113

"Yeah. Did he tell you about the creature?"

"A little. We'd rather hear it from you, though."

"You don't think it's crazy?"

"Do you?"

"I suppose I would."

"Agent Meyer and I like to keep an open mind."

"This your first time visiting Arrow Lake?"

"Actually, Agent Meyer and I were here about a year ago."

"A year ago. Yeah. That family disappeared on the other side of the lake. The Mathesons."

"That's right."

"So this is a follow up to see if the two are related?"

"Are they?"

"Maybe they are. I don't know anything about the Matheson family. They were weekenders. I ran into Dennis a couple times. Didn't know him really. I know about my neighbor, though, Hal Landon."

"Then let's just focus on that."

"Of course. Can I ask you a question?"

"Sure."

"You probably think, in your two visits, that Arrow Lake is simple."

"Is that a question?"

"Call it an assumption. You see the people, the village, you think it's simple."

"I don't know. Rustic. Agent Meyer likes the fish fry."

"Well. A lot of city people that come up here think it's simple, and it is, but I've lived here my whole life, eighty-eight years, and I'll tell you, there's more to the Arrow Lake than meets the eye."

"Give me an example."

"I'll get to that. Let me tell you what happened with Hal."

"All right. So what happened with Hal?"

"A few days before Hal's boy disappeared, I ran into him at the transfer station."

"What day of the week was that?"

"Um. That was a Saturday. The transfer station is open Wednesdays and weekends."

"My mother used to say that's where my father went to meet with the neighbors."

"I guess that's true everywhere. That Saturday I was dropping off the rose hips I dead headed. Hal had the leaves he'd gathered."

"And did you and Hal speak to each other?"

"Yeah, yeah. That was the start of the whole thing. Hal was telling me that the pike in the lake were taking out the ducks."

"The pike were eating the ducks?"

"That's what he thought. He didn't see it himself. He said he'd been on the other side of the house cleaning up the fall leaves he'd left in the tree line. He'd had his boys, Sam and Peter, gathering sticks, but they're only thirteen and ten, so they'd only managed to make it ten minutes before they disappeared to the little beach. So he was raking leaves, listening to that political channel, the one with that governor's brother, and after a while he realized that the children had gone suspiciously silent. Which usually means they're up to some trouble."

"That's usually the case."

"Right. So he walked around the house to check on the children and he finds the two boys standing on the incline near the water, one behind the other, both with dead stares out onto the lake. They told him they'd seen the ducks being pulled under."

"Sounds traumatic."

"I suppose. Hal said they were more fascinated than anything else, started rattling out questions and telling him what they thought it was. He told them that it might've been a large pike but the younger son, Peter, he said that it was an octopus."

"An octopus in Arrow Lake?"

"Ha, ha. Yeah. Hal explained to him that it's a freshwater lake and that octopuses live in saltwater. But the younger one, he insisted he saw a tentacle. Neither of the children wanted to go back into the water."

"And what did you tell him?"

"I told him it'd be best to keep the boys out of the lake for a while and best not over think it."

"So was it a pike or a pickerel?"

"I told him I didn't think it was a pike, but Hal said that the pickerel were way too small to pull a duck under, much less a dachshund—"

"Dachshund? A dog disappeared as well?"

"Yeah. Mary Wilkes, Hal's neighbor, she lost her little wiener dog, Barry. That morning she told Hal that Barry was missing and that she'd last seen him near the lake. Poor old guy was half blind, but he liked to swim. So to Hal's logic, ducks, a dachshund, it had to be pike."

"But you didn't think it was a pike?"

"No. No I didn't."

"What did you tell him it was?"

"I told him time to time there's something else in the lake."

"Something in the lake?"

"Beavers. Muskrats."

"Beavers and muskrats aren't going to pull down ducks. Maybe if they work together."

"No. Ha, ha. Hal said that too. But you know, a bobcat will pull a duck down, muskrat too, so why not a wiener dog. A lot of people don't realize big cats swim. Bobcats are the apex predator around here, you know."

"You thought it was a bobcat?"

"No. No I didn't. I just wanted the boys to stay out of the water without a ruckus, so that's what I told Hal. But it didn't make a difference."

"One of the boys did go back into the water."

"Or near it anyways. There's a tree over their little beach area, a red maple with a swing hanging from it. The young one, Peter, he likes to swing out over the water… Hal's wife said one minute the little guy was out there on the swing, the next he was gone, just disappeared. There were police diving teams, some local divers even helped out, but the body wasn't found."

"It says here they ran sonar, even dredged."

"Yeah. It's the brown water. The divers could only see so far in front of them, a yard or two maybe. Didn't matter, though, there's an underground river that runs beneath the lake."

"Underground river? Ah. Yes. It says right here that the diving team's sonar picked up a series of hollows."

"That's why they couldn't find the boy, or anyone else years past. When I was young it was just assumed that the lake, like many spring fed lakes, had a deep well in it, too deep to measure at the time. But on occasion, things lost in Arrow Lake would show up in one of the smaller neighboring lakes. They did a geological study and ran some deep-water dye experiment. Those hollows lead to vast caverns deep below the lake. They never found the boy, but there was little hope they would. I stopped in to check on Hal, found him sitting there gazing out his bay window. Hal had spent the three days staring at that lake, didn't sleep, probably didn't eat anything either, just kept staring."

"The report states he was under duress. Quite understandable. It also states that his wife Lydia took the older boy Sam to her parents. Leaving him alone—"

"Alone to stare into the abyss."

"You mean that in metaphor."

"Huh. The metaphor fits too. But no. I was referring to the fog that set in a day after the young one disappeared. Came in heavy, settling in from the coast. And there he was, no sleep, staring into it... I suppose the maxim has some merit—stare into the mist, it stares back. Because he was sure he saw something."

"What did he see?"

"Hal said he saw tentacles. Slithering around out there in the mist above the lake."

"Tentacles? Like the young one had said."

"Yeah. I told him that he'd been hallucinating. That he was seeing things out in the lake that just weren't there, seeing what he wanted see."

"But you knew better?"

"I did. I knew he saw something."

"What did you think Hal really saw out there in the mist?"

"Something. Something old. Something that comes around every forty years or so. I've seen it. Glimpses of it anyway. The tentacles, as long as a tree is high, slipping through the mist. It came when I was a boy, seven or eight. First a few animals went missing. Pets. The neighbor's dog, one of the goats the Jensens used to keep. Then people started disappearing. One after another, three in all, over the course of spring. No bodies, no nothing, gone without a clue. People were scared. My grandparents said that it, whatever it was, had been there since before the time of the Indians and that it woke on a cycle, every forty years or so. They told me to stay away from the lake, but I snuck down there. Saw the tentacles reflecting the silver of the moon, a knotted nest of them boiling the water, writhing in a slime in and around each other. I was scared stiff. Nightmares for years. But they were gone right after, and time went on without another disappearance... then sure enough, when I was late in my forties, pets started disappearing again. That spring I saw the water boil again, and that spring three more people went missing without a trace. That was forty years ago. Makes sense that it's back now."

"That many tentacles, could it be there's more than one? A hive waking like cicadas?"

"Could be. But in its presence, it feels…massive…and ancient. A magnitude of dark, suffocating evil. And there's something else. Did you notice any sadness when you got to the lake?"

"Well, a number of people were quite upset about the missing boy."

"No. I mean, inside of you. An empty ache, like there's a hole deep in your belly?"

"Now that you mention it, I have been distracted—but by nothing in particular."

"Exactly. Just feeling, a woeful feeling. See, when it comes, the whole of the lake sets with a sullen melancholy. And the closer you are, the deeper the ache. I felt it when I was a boy, again forty years ago, and I feel it now. The feeling of doom."

"Hrm. Excuse me. Um. Did you tell Hal Landon what you knew about the tentacles?"

"Not then. Not initially. I thought it best to cool him out. He hadn't slept, he wasn't thinking clear. But it didn't matter. He persisted. And against my advice, he decided to go looking for the creature."

"Alone? Is that the last time you saw him?"

"No. I wish it was. There wasn't anything I was going to say to keep him from going out into the fog, and when I realized trying to talk him out of it was as useless as talking Ahab out of searching for the mighty white whale, I came clean."

"You told him everything?"

"I told him what I knew, what I thought was out there. Told him again that there was no use even attempting to go up in front of that thing, but if he insisted, I'd go with him, on the condition he'd let me feed him and that we'd start fresh after he'd had some sleep. He agreed to eat and nap but he wanted me to wake him at midnight so we could go under the rise of the full moon… I was thinking that if I pushed him a day, he might catch his head. I'd brought a casserole with me and there was already a bunch of roasts and such in his icebox that the other neighbors had sent over. So, I heated up a plate and filled his belly. He passed out right there on the sofa, so I threw a blanket over him and headed back to my place to get some supplies, just in case."

"In case he woke up at midnight."

"Yes and no. I was thinking that after being up for so long, he might sleep for the next two days and by then it'd be too late to go out on the lake looking for that thing. But I wanted to make a good show of it when he did wake up, so I grabbed a couple of old iron trident fishing spears I had in the garage—they're seven-foot long—grabbed a speargun, an LED lantern, and my Winchester. Then I took all of that back to Hal's and sat there with him. I planned to move on to the guest room after a bit, but I fell asleep in the cushioned armchair, and next thing I know he's waking me up—it's half past eleven and there he is, bright and spry. I remember it was half past, because Hal's wife Lydia has three clockfaces there in the den. At any rate, like I said, when I woke up, he was spry and raring to go. I showed him what I brought, he added his handgun to the mix, and we took it down to the row boat."

"What kind of handgun was it?"

"I don't know the brand, Ruger maybe. Hal said it was a nine-millimeter. Anyway, by that time it was pretty bright out. I'm not saying you could read by the moonlight, but you could certainly see words on the page. The moon was full and the fog blanketing the lake was all lit up silver. The battery to the boat's electric motor was on the charger, so after we hauled the gear down, Hal had to run back for that while I stayed to stow everything. We had the two lanterns with us—both the LED kind with the white light—I hung one on a stick from the bow and put the other on the seat, but they were hurting the night vision rather than helping it, so I turned them off… Funny. In the moment, with hustling everything down there, the adrenalin and all, I kind of forgot about what we were doing there in the first place, but once I got everything stowed, and was just waiting there by myself, I heard the waves start to slosh up on the bank and that sick feeling I'd been carrying around became real intense, real quick. I mean, Hal couldn't have taken no more than three or four minutes running back to the garage, but time all but stopped. The water had been still, the waves were from something behind the fog, a wake, from something in the water. They grew in strength so that the aft of the boat started to rock, and the harder it rocked, the greater the dread, the hopelessness. I about lost my dinner when the waves abruptly stopped and the boat settled. Then Hal was there, dropping the battery into the back."

"Did you tell him? About the disturbance in the water?"

"No. I don't know why not. I guess I was in disbelief. Shock maybe. I mean I couldn't really believe we were getting into a ten-foot rowboat and heading out to find that thing. Everything in me was telling me we should be running in the opposite direction. But I didn't want him going out there alone."

"What was his state of mind?"

"Oh, he was giddy. Anxious. After we pushed away, he was leaning heavy from the till out into the fog, a look on his face like he was going to see his boy any minute."

"Not the monster?"

"No. It's clear to me now he was expecting we'd find his son. I suppose... I suppose he'd lost it already. And I was just seduced by his madness. Going out there with him somehow made sense at the time."

"But you did find it, didn't you?"

"Yeah. Or it found us. We must have made it pert near the center of the lake, the motor gently buzzing along, the mist wetting our faces as we passed through it. Out over the water that big full moon hung low and large, so close you could touch it—we could have been trolling a cloud. Then came the shadows. Fist sized dark spots moving all around us just behind the surface of the mist, so you could see them pass but not make out what they were. Then something a little more solid, a little more silver, like the back of a porpoise but long and thin, raced by the boat, disturbing the water, like the way a shark's dorsal cuts through the water, but closer to the surface like a snake... Hal stopped the motor, and the shadows continued to pass by, flying up over our heads, all around the boat, not circling, but we were in the midst, same with whatever was in the water. I could see the silver backs break the surface on both sides, creating enough wake to start us gently rocking. I picked up the Winchester, but Hal... Hal cried out for his son. *'Peter,'* he said in a whisper. *'Peter, we're here for you.'* I shushed him, to shut him up, but he persisted. *'Peter, Peter...'* Then that feeling again, that dread, it came back full on, and maybe that was good, because the look on Hal's face changed. There was no doubt he felt it too and was starting to snap out of his delusion of finding Peter out there, and when the first of those shadows buzzing the boat veered close enough to reveal itself, he was awake."

"Revealed itself?"

"To be a tentacle, upright like a cobra, silver skinned, the size of a light post. Hal's demeaner changed tout sweet. He called it a son-of-a-bitch, grabbed one of the seven-foot iron tridents we brought along, and swung it up, almost hitting me with the barbs in the process. The tentacle was wriggling around, the tip dipping and dangling overhead, probing maybe, just kind of hanging in the air over the edge of the boat, close enough to see the suckers. Hal poked up at it with the spear, but with being in a boat and the tentacle moving to and fro, his first attempts to stab it were clumsy, and rather than connect with the point, he ended up slapping the steel rod against it. And it reacted immediately on contact. Another tentacle flew up close to the first. Then another. See, I figure it wasn't the sound of him calling out for Peter that had attracted them, but a tactile alert, first of the boat in the water, and then the slap of that iron spear, and when Hal finally did harpoon one of those tentacles, we had the creature's full attention."

"What happened?"

"Well, all we were seeing were the tips of those tentacles, all three stretched up out of the water, growing from the size of light posts to telephone poles. Then the boat itself was thrust upward and we found ourselves on a sea of them. It was as if we were in the center of a lake of silver trees—not a hive, but one giant tentacled monster, the arms, twenty, thirty, forty feet long, writhing all around us in every direction… In my memory, the image, it's ah…spectacular, beautiful even, but at the time, it was terrifying. I was…frozen in horror. You see, when the boat was thrust up, I'd slipped back off the bench seat into the cradle of the bow. I tucked snug on my back, legs up, just holding the Winchester out from my waist as the boat rocked forward-back, side-to-side. And it wasn't just the horror, but the dread, hopelessness, I lost all will to fight. To move at all. Huh. I didn't realize it right then, but I wet myself."

"And Hal Landon? Was he frozen too?"

"Oh no sirree. Hal was raging. He seemed to be immune to the dread. I suppose, grieving for Peter, he'd used up all his sadness—no, not used up—become accustomed to it. The whole time I was paralyzed with fear, Hal was there battling the beast. Stabbing at those long silver tentacles as they swung down toward him, dodging, stabbing, kicking them away. It was futile really, swinging at the two or three tentacles near his end of the boat while we were suspended and surrounded by who knows how many others, too many to count. But he was relentless, relentless as Don Quixote. He got some whacks in, lost one of the tridents then went at it with the other, but…"

"But?"

"But… Hurting that thing. Stopping it. It was never going to happen. I'm glad he had his chance to scream at the beast. I'm sure it was much more of a stand than little Peter or any of its other victims ever had. But like I said, it was futile from the beginning. It all ended rather quick really. As if the beast had tired of him, or maybe it really did take a few swings to home in on him, because as soon as one of those long arms came in contact with him, two others followed. The first grabbed his leg, and he got maybe two stabs into it before the next two had slithered around his torso. Then they just pulled him from the boat, and they all disappeared. The boat dropped like a rock, slammed into the water. And I just stayed there, huddled in the bow, the Winchester in my hands."

"Mr. Westerhausen, Nate, Angus told us that you stayed in the boat all night."

"And into a good part of the next day. I figured that the reason the creature attacked Hal was because he was moving, the tactile thing, I figured, it must be blind. So I didn't move a muscle, couldn't have if I wanted to. I waited for a wind to pick up and send the boat drifting to shore, and me with it. Fortunately, it did, or I might still be out there."

"The report stated that you were the one to come forward to report Hal's disappearance."

"I reported what happened. They called it a disappearance. I believe they're still out there, combing the lake."

"Angus says that they're waiting for the fog to lift, it's supposed to as early as later today, or tomorrow."

"They won't find anything."

"I don't suppose they will. Not if there's an underground river that washes everything away."

"You know, that must be where it goes. Down to some deep lair to sleep for forty years."

"It's an interesting theory. One that makes sense."

"You don't believe me, do ya?"

"Nate, I told you when we sat down, we're here to listen, and to help. That means we're not here to judge you or any anything you share with us today. The sole purpose of this interview is to gather information in aid of the of the investigation of the disappearance of Hal Landon and his ten-year-old son Peter."

"But you must think I'm crazy. I'm not, I assure you. There's something down there."

"Mr. Westerhausen, I understand your frustration, but surely it has occurred to you, that short of the discovery of a new technology that can allow a diver or a camera down into an underground river that deep, or a change in the creature's habits, we'll have to wait forty years to find out."

40
Tales from the
CANYONS of
the DAMNED
FEATURING
STEVE ODEN
CHARLES BAROUCH
HUNTER C. EDEN
PRESENTED BY USA TODAY BESTSELLING AUTHOR
DANIEL ARTHUR SMITH

Bloody Bridge

Steve Oden

The Scottish terrier toy was smartly turned out in kilt, belt, and beribboned tunic. His velveteen curls had been teased. Black eyes were bright with enthusiasm and intelligence. The dog held himself at attention without the quiver of a whisker in his neatly trimmed-and-waxed beard.

All-Sector Commander Toy Soldier nodded at the prim and proper officer, wondering if his reputation as the leader of a formidable fighting force was well-founded. He seemed too officious and concerned with appearance.

"At ease, Colonel McCallan. Please be seated."

"Thankee, sirrah. Everyone calls me Mac." The thick burr in his voice made him difficult to understand, another point to take up. They didn't want an excitable colonel shouting in Gaelic over the radio.

"Well, Mac. You've been briefed on what the supreme commander needs from your war dogs. I want to answer any questions, hear your recommendations, and offer you the chance to voice objections."

The terrier sat with barely contained energy, eyes flashing. He answered, "None, none, and none, sirrah!"

"You mean there is nothing you'd change about the overall strategy and tactics we must use to capture the bridge? It doesn't bother you that, for a period of time, your brigade will have enemy forces in front of and behind you?"

The response was a growl of confidence. "Naw... The lads and lasses will execute yer orders an' be waiting with teapots boiling an' bangers frying when relief arrives. You just leave it tae the war dogs, Sirrah!"

Toy Soldier didn't know whether to laugh at the bravado or start looking for another unit leader. This one might be crazy. But something about Col. Mac reminded him of another warrior. She never shied away from a challenge and threw herself into bloody chaos because she trusted her own instincts and her teammates.

In the end, that had been her undoing. Fairy Princess was gone, and he had loved her. There hadn't even been a body to mourn and bury. Just the burned-out hulk of a lightly armored reconnaissance vehicle.

For a time, he blamed the blind bear until understanding dawned. He realized it had been the only possible way to victory. The bear had ordered her unsupported attack on entrenched enemy positions, knowing it was a suicide mission. Her courage resulted in the enemy shifting forces and going on the defensive instead of attacking.

The hurt was a raw wound that might never heal, worse than any battle injury he had suffered. Now, he was prepared to order another brave, proud soldier into a situation where his war dogs would be outnumbered and forced to defend on two fronts.

"Och, sirrah. 'Tis a great honor fer the brigade tae get this mission. Ah give you ma pledge that we'el skelp them green-skinned toadies and pettet-lipped bairns, or ma name's not Rudolphus Hector McCallan!"

The terrier leaped to his feet and growled a Gaelic curse on all enemies of the Free Toys.

This time, Toy Soldier couldn't help the grin on his face.

"I guess you'll do, Mac," he said, convinced the same pride and courage ran through the colonel's veins that had motivated his princess.

Count Thaddeus monitored the fight from his command trailer parked among a battery of missile launchers. Per his orders, troops were falling back, putting up just enough resistance to keep the demons from sweeping down the road. Mortars, missiles, and artillery rained hot steel down on the attackers, bleeding them for every meter of advance.

His intelligence gatherers had been woefully inaccurate with their force estimates. Instead of poorly coordinated small guerilla units, they faced at least two self-supporting regiments, several thousand savage fighters, with automatic weapons and shoulder-fired RPGs, willing to swarm in suicide attacks against AI-piloted fighting machines.

No threat to his Tri-tracks, of course. The goal of the fighting retreat was to get the demons concentrated on the flat ground in front of the bridge, out in the open with no ruins or rubble for protection. The Count would call in air strikes and wipe out the opposition while sending two flying, armored columns around the flanks to complete the entrapment.

Assault against the Free Toys would be indefinitely delayed. He needed time to build back strength and replenish munitions.

"Sir, the last armored unit is pulling back across the bridge. Our soldiers and mech brigades have occupied prepared defense positions on the far side of the river. Distance between them and the approaching enemy is sufficient for a safety buffer," reported a subaltern.

"Send the green signal to our bombers. I want to see a square mile of fire and ash out there when they're finished!"

The Count turned to his strategy coordinator. "Get the flanking movements underway. Tell them to make all possible speed to close the back door."

His Tri-tracks would be ferried across the river to trap the demons between the outpost and bridge.

He reminded his staff of an important standing order for the upcoming attack.

"This is a black flag mission. No quarter, no prisoners," he said. "I want those monstrosities ground into pulp!"

"The task force has been assembled, and the war dogs are prepared to jump off at your order, sirrah. Toy Soldier is in the field to personally lead the relief column," Pachy reported to the blind bear.

The supreme commander would never feel comfortable directing movements of armies on expansive battlefields. His tactical mistakes could mean the deaths of thousands of loyal Free Toy fighters and possibly failure of the cause.

Risk was a necessary component of the struggle. The bear had already wasted lives, not intentionally but because he saw the opportunity to grab victory from the jaws of defeat.

Those he sent into the firestorm willingly accepted their orders and were proud to have been chosen. Their commander, however, lived with guilt. The blood on his paws couldn't be washed away.

The panoramic monitor in the command center showed a view of the contested bridge.

Fog almost obscured the structure. Only the top masts of the suspension cable supports were visible to the war dogs parasailing toward the target. The assault had been planned when the river's water temperature and early morning dewpoint created a thick morning mist that wouldn't clear until burned away by the sun.

Bear paced as the first airborne combat companies disappear in the fog. The follow-on troops and specialty support units waited until a green flare burst overhead. The attackers had secured both ends of the bridge and attached climbing ropes that dangled into the river.

The parasailers dived into the water, cut loose from their wings, and grabbed the ropes. A trained group of diving dogs helped their fellow troopers. Larger parasails loaded with munitions, radio equipment, and a mobile field hospital splashed down and immediately inflated into rubber boats. War dogs climbed aboard and shot grappling hooks to the bridge so the precious supplies could be hauled up.

Finally, the diving dogs disappeared under the surface. They mined the vital bridge foundations so the span could be destroyed, ensuring that neither enemy could reclaim it.

Col. McCallan was the first dog down, a gesture that helped cement his reputation for bravery but which the supreme commander thought ill-advised—until he recalled never liking to lead soldiers from the rear.

Before his paws hit the bridge, the colonel's reports on enemy reaction to the assault helped the blind bear arrange his battle board. The crucial observation so far was that his dogs received only small-arms fire from the kingdom's side of the river, and no armor seemed to be moving forward yet.

The opposite side was quiet, probably due to carpet bombing from aircraft that had left the bridge approach a patchwork of craters and mangled demons.

Before he landed, Col. McCallan had keyed his microphone with the "successful-landing-and-bridge-capture" code. He swooped low in his parasail and uttered a barking battle cry that was answered by 800 howls from his war dogs.

"The fools!"

Voodoo Doll surveyed the field of carnage in front of the bridge with satisfaction. The strategy employed by Count Thaddeus had solved one of her problems. She had released throngs of reserve demons to dig with claws, improvised shovels, even fangs, if necessary, to tunnel among the craters and occupy them under the pall of fog, smoke, and dust.

"It's the perfect opportunity for infiltration, to get close and overwhelm the enemy at close quarters," she told her subordinate. "Make certain we reach the bridge before the overcast clears and they can see us!"

She also had reports that the kingdom's armored assets were executing a pincer maneuver on the flanks.

"Fine, I couldn't have hoped for a better outcome," she hissed. "Their strength is on the sides. Nothing left in the middle except infantry. We will go straight up the gut and seize them by the throat."

Voodoo Doll cackled and urged her demons onward.

"I can't believe it!" Count Thaddeus growled.

He barely credited initial reports that an assault force had taken the bridge and was keeping his infantry and the demons at bay. Then, a scout squad sent video of barricades bristling with automatic weapons, mortars, and fighters waving rebel banners. They resembled curly-haired dogs but fought like rabid animals.

If there was any justice, he thought, the Voodoo Doll's guerillas were also stymied. They had occupied bomb and shell craters; but when the river mist burned away, they became sitting ducks for the rebel snipers and machine gunners.

Somehow, the dogs had even managed to parachute in a pair of field howitzers.

The bridge had become a death trap at both ends. But it was too valuable to yield. He had to get it back, whatever the cost.

"Your orders, sir?" asked his new and untried field marshal.

The Count sighed. "Order the armored columns to return and rejoin our ground forces. I want the tanks to lead a coordinated attack across the bridge. We will wipe out the rebels and consolidate on the other side before hunting down what is left of the demons."

He ignored the field marshal's salute and barked another command. "I also want the Voodoo Doll's head on a platter! See to it personally."

Col. Rudolphus Hector McCallan patrolled the bridge, encouraging his toy Scotty dogs with howling curses and threats at the enemies on both sides. They'd beaten back three major counterattacks. Losses were relatively light so far because Count Thaddeus dared not use heavy artillery or energy weapons for fear of damaging the valuable span.

The demons on the other side had been repeatedly repulsed by close-combat canine fighters like they had never encountered. The Scotties could smell them out, attack with sharp teeth and wicked blades, and had the advantage of snipers perched above in the bridge's overhead structure.

"Keepin' their heads down, I see." The colonel chuckled as a marksman took out another demon who had carelessly peered over the edge of a shell hole.

"Blowin' their ruddy heads off, more like it, suh!" said a scruffy female sergeant with a snarling grin. "I hope after dark ye'll let me send out teams to do some bladework in them holes and debris piles. Just a suggestion, o' course."

"Patience, m' lass. We'll see what develops."

Col. McCallan's worry was not the efficiency of his fighters but the current state of the ammunition reserve. They'd lost one of the inflatable boats and all its contents. The extra rifle ammo, cannon shells, and road mines were gone.

The shrewd commander had bunkered both ends of the bridge, then thrown out skirmishers to occupy the rubble and derelict buildings on the kingdom's side. His heavy mortars and "hell-puppy" howitzers were in battery, zeroed on the approaches armor would have to take. The two cannons could be depressed to fire anti-personnel shells or elevated for pinpoint targeting of enemy tanks or counter-battery salvoes.

No artillery except light mortars, grenade launchers, and shoulder-fired RPGs defended the other end of the bridge. The fighting there had been close-in and often paw-to-claw. McCallan didn't expect it to change.

Things were going passably well now, but one more kingdom counterattack might elevate the situation to a crisis for his battalion. He whipped his baton up to salute the war dogs around him. They growled and howled like blood wolves as he marched off, worrying about how long they could hold before he had to order the bridge blown.

Then would come a fighting retreat, and he wondered what that would feel like. His war dogs had never backed away from a battle, but those were his orders.

Toy Soldier had learned from his mentor, the blind bear. The most important reality of the battlefield was that best-laid plans never survived first contact with the enemy. Tacticians who thought otherwise were fools.

The strategy he developed for relief of the Scottish battalion had three facets. None were necessarily dependent on the others so that victory or defeat wouldn't hinge on the failure of one of the moving parts.

His commander had approved, even found some humor in the approach.

"The war dogs are hanging on by their teeth now, no pun intended. Their sacrifice has allowed us to move assets into position and prepare," said the bear.

Toy Soldier rode in an armored personnel carrier, part of the column of carefully shepherded assault vehicles that the rebellion possessed. Most had come with Santos von Clauswitz's surrendered brigade.

Heavy equipment and artillery had always been in short supply for the toys and their allies. At the rear rolled three obsolete tanks, formerly owned by the children's kingdoms but disabled by the rebel toys.

The vehicles were pieced back together with welds, rivets, and prayers. They looked like junk, with rusty carapaces, scorch marks, and patches. But the guns worked, and the carefully trained tank teams were inordinately proud of their steeds.

Toy Soldier had been forced to tie a scarf around his face. Dust and smoke were thick and the smell awful. Contested ground always stank like an abattoir, but this was worse. There was nothing for it, though. He turned in the hatch and pointed the column forward with a pumping gesture that meant to open throttles and make the best possible speed.

The war dogs braced for another—probably the primary—counterattack from the kingdom side. Eye-in-the sky drones spotted an echelon of heavy armor led by tri-tracked tanks barreling toward the bridge. Enemy ground troops had pulled back to give the war machines plenty of room.

The Scotty dog brigade's two hell-puppies were plunging fire toward the tanks. The light, portable field pieces could only knock out such behemoths with lucky shots.

Col. McCallan had pulled back his skirmishers and snipers. He'd also done a hasty reorganization of the bridge defenses, shifting the RPG squads to the end where he expected an armored blitzkrieg.

He looked down on the disposition of forces from a type of crow's nest that had been cobbled together for him at the top of the tallest bridge pillar. At hand was a rifle, portable radio, and his flask of whiskey.

To the east, he could see a massive cloud of dust thrown up by the enemy armor, highlighted by flashes of exploding shells from his two-cannon battery. The west seemed quiet, with no movement evident in the no-man's land of craters and ripped earth.

Instinct informed him that something was going on there also. He had sent a message to the sergeant to be on highest alert. The colonel tipped the flask toward the west, hopeful the relief column was on its way. He swigged and wondered if this might be his final toast.

Voodoo Doll sensed the battlefield portents. The dog soldiers were ferocious. They had held off her demons all day. Intuition—not magic—informed her that now was the time for an all-out thrust, sending her remaining demons directly at the rebels who held fast to the bridge.

The time to conquer was at hand. She would lead them herself. Back from the dead, the feeder of flesh to her faithful, she was unafraid despite her pitiful, lumpy body.

She made her way through crooked trenches where her demons stood respectfully. They were hungry for victory and fresh meat, but awed that Voodoo Doll would be at the head of the attack. She ordered complete silence and gestured them to follow.

When a taller demon stood straight to let her pass, a fleshy whap and spurt of green blood from his head marked a sniper's bullet. The body slid down the muddy trench wall. Voodoo Doll reached out a malformed hand and smeared the blood and brain matter on her face.

An electric current went through the demons behind her. They passed their companion's corpse and reached out sharp claws to baptize themselves in gore. Soon there was nothing left of the dead fighter except guts and raw bones.

"Count Thaddeus, the Tri-tanks have deployed in staggered line and are almost at the bridge entrance," reported his radio technician.

The count's saturnine features showed no excitement. There was still much to do to secure the bridge—and demons on the other side, although the Voodoo Doll's guerilla fighters had been depleted in numbers and effectiveness.

"Transmit: Do not use HE rounds. I repeat, no high-explosive shells! I don't want structural damage to the bridge. Also, the shock troops need to be right behind the tanks so they can swarm the defensive positions," he instructed.

Squawking speakers, barked orders, and the outside racket of missile launchers lofting death could not interrupt the Count's thoughts. No surprises this time, simply overwhelming force in a battle that could bring other kingdoms to his banner.

They needed a leader to defeat the toys and other potential upstarts in this fractured world. Someone who could put things right, once and for all.

This action would be decisive, and he would win.

The crackling of rifle fire announced that the war dogs had contact with demon forces at the west end of the bridge. Col. McCallan trained his binoculars toward the smoke and debris as a heavy automatic weapon began to pump death, silencing the hungry roars of attackers with a steady thump-thump-thump of high-caliber explosive rounds.

His radio pinged with an update. "Suh, the tanks are firing anti-personnel rounds only. Guess the bastards don't want to damage the bridge. Infantry coming up too, with some AI-controlled walkers. We ain't pulling back. Gonna get 'em by the throat and hold on!"

The colonel's heart swelled with pride. The Scotties would fight to the last dog.

Shaking dirt from his thick, curly coat, the war dog finally conceded that the relief column would be too late. His sappers had their orders.

When what was left of his brigade went over the sides into the water, he'd give a signal for explosive charges to be triggered.

"Wish't we had the pipes," he told himself remorsefully. He had ordered brigade pipers to leave their unwieldy instruments behind so they could carry more ammunition. The skirling of bagpipes before the bridge blew would be a fitting paw-in-the-eye for the enemy.

The leader of the Scotties licked the iron sights of his rifle and aimed through a gap in the wreckage where kingdom soldiers would pass. "Steady on," he whispered. "Steady on…"

An earsplitting noise nearly shook him off his perch. Fiery arcs shot overhead, causing him to conclude Count Thaddeus had deployed missiles to mop up the demon guerillas after his dogs had thrown them back.

"Cheeky bastard," the colonel growled.

Then, he beheld that the missiles were actually man-shaped, and they wielded wire-guided, anti-tank weapons. The kingdom's Tri-tracks began to disappear in gouts of fire.

"Rocket men," he said, amazed.

Part of the relief had arrived in time. The sky swarmed with red hurtling rockets, strapped to the backs of fliers who wore pointed helmets and thick suits with oxygen tanks on their thighs.

Some of the rocket men swooped low to strafe Count Thaddeus's infantry in a precision display of machine-gunnery. Others dropped fragmentation bombs. Still other fliers attacked the kingdom's propeller-powered war planes, nimbly darting around them until the sky filled with burning aircraft.

McCallan stood and danced a jig, yelling the brigade's Gaelic war cry into the radio. Translated, it meant: "Sons of the hounds, come and get your flesh!" A howling huzzah from below meant the counterattack was already underway.

Three things Toy Soldier thought he'd never witness occurred when he threw his forward units at the demons massed to attack the bridge.

The first was a charging spearhead of heavy horses, their riders encased in silvery armor with lances couched. They held embossed shields of the Free State of Saxony, with a sable-green-yellow coat of arms. A forest of swords waved with sharp points and razor edges.

The knights' mission was to root out the demons in trenches, craters, and debris.

The second sight was an aerial display of one-man whirligigs. Shaped like dragonflies, the acrobatic fighters darted almost like the insects. Every dip ended with the release of smart grenades, phosphorous bombs, and poison darts on the hapless demons. Like the rocket men, the whirligigs were red and emblazoned with the insignia of the Free State of Beijing.

The most startling image that fixed itself in Toy Soldier's mind happened when he led the armored personnel carriers onto the bridge to reinforce the Scotty Brigade. Hand-to-hand fighting now raged, but the demons were too few and leaderless.

Voodoo Doll had disappeared in the furious counterattack of war dogs and combat toys. Soon, her dispirited followers began to slink away. They'd be hunted down and eliminated, but Toy Soldier wanted the ugly doll, first and foremost.

In a moment that occurs on all battlefields, when the roar of death and destruction subsides and blood-crazed soldiers come to their senses, Toy Soldier looked up. High above in the suspension structure, a small figure glared down with hatred. Crudely sewn and lumpy, the thing hurled invective at him.

"There!" he shouted, pointing. "It's the doll. Get her!"

Instead of fleeing, Voodoo Doll fumbled at herself with blunt hands. She had no weapon that Toy Soldier could see. Was she grasping for poison to kill herself? Instead, a vertical slit opened from chest to belly, and something squirmed out.

The burlap husk fell away, revealing a naked female form.

As she prepared to dive into the river, Toy Soldier used his helmet battle camera to focus on the figure. It revealed striations of infected scars from her scalp down the sides of her body. But the face–oh, the face he knew and loved–was recognizable.

The small figure who had once been Fairy Princess leaped, plunged, and gracefully entered the muddy water with barely a splash. She was gone, and the veteran commander wished he had never seen what was hidden in the costume.

Not because of defaced beauty or horror of the encounter, but because he realized they had not searched the wreckage of her reconnaissance vehicle closely enough. They assumed she was dead inside: mangled, burned, and made one with the machine.

This was the excuse for not recovering the body. Instead, they honored her sacrifice and bravery by memorializing heroic actions that might have saved the rebellion.

He should have performed the due diligence that Princess deserved. He wondered how long she had suffered, trapped in the pyre of scorched and ripped ceramic armor, aluminum, and plastic that had been her scout vehicle, the Magic Pony.

Toy Soldier's broken heart twisted and ached as it never had before. He sensed that the insane princess would be seen and heard from again. Damaged inside and out, she desired revenge and reckoning.

She was the enemy of the Free Toys and their allies. Worse still, her thoughts toward him were black and cold.

Toy Soldier held it all inside while Scotty dogs and armored knights celebrated around him. They had earned the victory, a potentially conflict-changing battle. But to him, the child kingdoms were no longer the enemy.

He now must fight against someone he loved more than himself.

Gibberlings

Charles Barouch

It's the height of summer. Staying indoors is driving me mad. I'm so tired of the new rules. It isn't about disagreeing with them. They aren't arbitrary, they're written in blood. Still, I want to stand on a street corner at noon just to feel the sun, the heat off the roads, see the glare on the shop windows. I miss shop windows in daylight.

Six months ago, I took all of that for granted. We all did. People complained about the noise, the traffic, and the latest crop of city-folk moving into our sleepy little town. Back then, I was the one reminding folk that our town was dying, that these newcomers were saving what was left, not burying it. That was the stupid, useless sort of things we worried about back before.

Then, on a Tuesday morning, they were suddenly here. Not an influx of new people. No, these things aren't people. Not remotely like us. And when they attacked, they didn't show a preference between recent arrivals or town elders. They didn't discriminate by race or age or gender. They ate everyone they could reach.

News had no mention of them.

Whatever they were, we were the only beneficiaries of their attention.

We call them the Gibberlings because of the sound they make. The sound they make when their mouths are empty. The other sound, the one when their mouths are full… it rings in my ears even when I'm locked away safe.

We figured out the rules quickly. They are short and have three legs, so we climb better than they do. They have no hands, so doorknobs are a barrier. Individually, they are weak and slow. They hate darkness and hide all night. Best of all, water destroys them.

That last one, we thought that was our answer. The town spent an evening, we really came together—worked together—and I got every lawn sprinkler and fire hydrant and anything, even water balloons, set and ready. Dawn came and we hit them with all of it. Nature even complied. There was a torrential rainstorm.

They do this thing when the water hits. It sounds like a sizzle, like water hitting a hot pan, but they don't burn. They freeze. They freeze then crack then fall to pieces. For one of us, a person who has seen the horror of them eating people and pets and farm animals, it was beautiful. If you can't understand that it's because you've been lucky enough to never have faced the Gibberlings.

It was a moment of victory, a day of celebration. The streets were clear of them. The next morning there were just as many. And it wasn't that they rose from the shards of their dead, we swept the sidewalks clean. And they didn't wander in from outside the perimeter of water. They were just there. It was as if the rays of the rising sun spawned them. Short, mottled-skinned, hungry, and slow, they roamed the sidewalk. If we had been braver, they would have eaten us all. We weren't. Everyone greeted the sun that day from indoors. We watched, hoping, until first light.

The weight of our failure was unbearable.

That was then. Today will be different, at least for me. It's nearly two hours before first light. I am outside. I choose to be outside. I am going to feel the sun, not by leaning out a window, not by standing with my face pressed to glass. And I assure you this isn't suicide by monster. There's a plan here. I intend to survive in defiance of the creatures.

When I was a kid, my family used to picnic by Kaisen Lake. I don't remember it, we stopped going when my mom died. I was three. There are pictures, though. My mom took hundreds of pictures during those five brief years that she and dad went up to picnic and row and recharge.

Since she was usually behind the camera, I only have one or two of her. No selfies for my mom. She didn't do that. So I decided to free myself of the rules up here at the lake. It was an hour's drive. If the Gibberlings destroy the car, and they've been known to mass up on objects and break them with their combined weight, I can hike back at night. If not, I'll have an easy trip after.

The lake itself is my safety. I'm on an inner tube, smack dab in the middle of the water. They have no technology, no ropes, no bridges, no flying-what-have-yous. In a world full of monsters, I will brave the daylight and feel the sun with nothing to protect me but the tube, my bathing suit, and the countless gallons of Kaisen Lake.

I watch the sun rising, that traitorous morning star.

For the first time, I get an eye-level view of the Gibberlings. They really are spawned–or summoned, or phased into our world, or... I don't know really–by the kiss of those rays. Not there in the dark. Appearing in the sunlight. Flashlights don't call them up. My headlights on the ride up here summoned none of them. They are creatures of the sun. Banished when it departs, back when it arrives.

There's been theories like that. Now I have proof. I'm sure others have already confirmed it. Hell, everybody has video equipment nowadays. If it's been done, no one shared their findings with me.

Slowly, they start massing up into little clumps, here and there, along the edge of the water. The monsters seem to know, to sense me, immediately. It's just another odd thing about our tiny little apocalypse.

In the movies, the disease or zombie or whatever, creates a breakdown of society. This wasn't that. The nights are safe. Buildings are safe. We've just shifted our schedules and kept the lights on. My apartment has power. I have Wi-Fi. Phone towers need replacing more often but our phones still work.

Of all the ways for the world to end, this might be the most civil.

If they expand out, humans will be culled but not extinguished in a single, brutal rush. Our death will come. Too many food animals will go. Too many fields will be trampled during the day. Rooftop gardens will be enough for a while, especially once the mass of humanity has been severely reduced.

I go back to watching the shore.

One runs into the water. Splash. Sizzle. Freeze. Shatter. Sink.

Another tries. Same sequence.

They want me.

This time of year, they have fourteen hours, maybe sixteen, to accomplish their goal. The online almanac says sundown is at eight forty-five. But there are no mountains here, just a large, flat area. So, I suspect that they'll get a little extra time from that.

I'm not worried.

I have a small waterproof bag tied to my waist. It dangles below the inner tube and holds my cold drinks and a little food. I've fasted before, I don't really need the food. The water, however, is both hydration and defense. Not that I'll need the second part of that equation. The lake is teeming with protection.

The other things in my bag are a cell phone, in its own waterproof case, and some sunscreen. Even if I hadn't been shut-in for six months, skin can burn. In this brave new world, maybe I should skip the sunscreen and wear the burn as a trophy. Practicality demands that I use it, though. So, I probably will.

Another splash and sizzle. Then another.

Most of the groups are just milling about. The risk-takers, the ones diving in and dying, all seem to be from one group on the east side of the lake. Not all the ones on that side, just one small group.

I start watching for a pattern.

Boredom is already starting to set in. This idea, it was brilliant when I came up with it. It was rebellious and powerful. The reality? Less so. Fourteen or sixteen hours of anything is hard to do. The penalty for leaving early is death, so here I float, watching the Gibberlings commit suicide and knowing they'll be back to full strength tomorrow.

East to west, the lake is a quarter mile across. The monsters can jump but I've never heard of one that can best seven or eight feet. Some of the ones in that insane little pack are taking running jumps. Under three feet by what I can see. Unimpressive.

I watch for a while but even their deaths, and their desire for my death, gets boring after a while. I pull up the bag and put on some sunscreen. As I look down into the water, I can see that there's no sign of fish. Somehow the Gibberlings have gotten them, too. Perhaps some cagey ones are still safe, hiding during the day. All I know is this lake used to be filled with schools of all sorts. The park rangers had a devil of a time chasing off fishermen. The lake was protected back then.

Now it's protecting me.

After I reseal the bag and put it away in the water, I look back at the shoreline. Still just the one group trying. That's when something new occurs. In all my sightings, from my window, in all the videos people have shared, I've never seen one so big. It's the size of a large horse. The three-legged structure of their bodies is ill suited to his bulk. The creature wobbles as it walks, a crazy, drunken, lurching motion.

One of the others stood between it and the lake. Bulky pushes it in. Splash. Sizzle. Freeze. Shatter. Sink.

Then Bulky sits back and sweeps a leg forward, shoving another Gibberling into the water. Then another. There is a glint on the water. I thought it was the sun reflected through a bit of the spray that was thrown up by Bulky's actions, but quickly realize it wasn't. The glint remains steady as he pushes another into the lake. No, it doesn't remain, it grows slightly.

The other groups move toward the big beast. They are lining up to be pushed. It is the opposite of what we think of with every species on Earth. They are volunteering for death.

Splash. Sizzle. Freeze. Shatter. Sink. Over and over again.

The glint grew bigger, more glaring. A few more go in and I begin to understand. The ones being pushed in, they left a tiny bit of cold as they died. The glint is growing bigger because the ice is expanding. It is just a matter of time. The patch is getting larger, the lake isn't. They have enough hours to make it to the middle.

I start to paddle a bit to the west. That's when I see another group forming there as well. Another group pushing members in and building their own path. It isnt' just the end for me. This is the end of humanity. I float alone in the middle of Kaisen Lake and say aloud the words that would be humankind's epitaph: "The Gibberlings are learning."

Under Denver
Hunter C. Eden

Everybody wants to talk about the airport: the secret Illuminati hangars, the Satanic murals, the big blue demon horse statue out front...yeah, it's weird, I guess. In a *tourist* kind of way. Fly back to Nebraska or wherever and tell them you stood in the beating heart of the New World Order. Maybe call into Alex Jones. Poser.

I'm a third-gen Colorado native. Here's what they don't tell you:

Downtown, we've got a skyscraper called the Auraria Tower. The top of it looks like a cash register, and the inside is mostly banks, coffeeshops, one or two restaurants, and a couple oil companies. No Satan murals, no blue demon horse statue, no secret hangars. But if you go down to the bottom level of the parking garage, there's a scuffed-up metal door with a concrete staircase going down. I used to work in the Auraria Tower as a barista, and I accidentally went through that door coming off my evening shift one night. I was down there a long time.

Floor -1 is the Night Bank. It's run by the mob, but it's got tellers, checking accounts, and even its own credit card—*There are some things— like your kneecaps—that money can't buy. For everything else, there's NostraCard.* I got hired at the Night Bank as a teller but fucked up counting my drawer one night. Not like a *whack you and bury you alive* fuck-up but definitely a *you won't be walking again* fuck-up. So, I ran downstairs before my *capo* could sit me down for a performance review.

Credit's not hard to get at the Night Bank, unless you live on Floor -2 with the Nazis. Their applications get rejected every time since they took out those flying saucer loans and defaulted. My Ancestry results convinced them I was white enough to couch-surf in the Fourth Reich's lobby, but they still made me do all the chores. You ever scrub Nazi toilets? The Master Race has surprisingly bad aim.

I couldn't go back upstairs because of the Mob, but after a couple months of that I was desperate enough to try going downstairs. *Oberfuhrer* Günther wouldn't let anyone go down there, but one night I managed to steal his keys and sneak past the door. Floor -3 is where the cannibals live. They found the perfect place to do it, too, right where the natural caverns begin. You go from well-thumbed copies of *Mein Kampf* and swastika tea doilies to dripping granite caves with heads spiked on stakes and bodies being roasted on giant spits. You like locally sourced? You like the Paleo diet? So did these fuckers, and there's nothing as Paleo as eating your fellow man.

But they respected my veganism. One or two of them would poke me and say I was organic and grain-fed, but when you have a floor of SS officers fattened up on strudel and spaetzle just above you, that's just not much of a temptation. Everybody hates Nazis—unless they're free-range.

Of course, there was nothing for me to eat there, so I took my chances on the stairs down to Floor -4, the glowing fungus gardens where the Reptilians live. Floor -4 is the last vestige of their Mesozoic Empire, the only surviving outpost after their apocalyptic world war—the one that killed the dinosaurs. I guess that would be World War 0? World War .5? I don't know. But I do know that looking into their cold, lidless eyes, watching as forked tongues licked slaver off rows of flesh-cutting teeth, I had a sudden realization that banking for the mob and cleaning Nazi toilets weren't the worst directions your life could go. So, I ran as they slithered after me. I threw myself behind the door, locked it, and started composing my apology to the *Oberfuhrer*.

Then I realized that this wasn't Floor -3 again. I'd taken the wrong stairwell, down to Floor -5. The smell and whispering voices and the greasy sheen of obscene flesh in my iPhone's light…I stood there, sickened. I don't know how long. It might have been hours. It might have been days. It might have been months or even years as the Antediluvian Ones rose up around me like monoliths of flesh, their thousand eyes mirrors of horror, their voices symphonies of madness.

What do you want? they said in one whispering, howling torrent of words.

"I want to go back to the surface," I said. "No more Nazis and cannibals and lizard people and—and whatever the fuck you are."

Laughter seemed to ring from the very atoms around me, then I was back up here in Denver. Lost my girlfriend, my kids, my car, my job, my apartment, and all my savings. Like I said, I'd been down there a long time, and to get me back up to the surface, the Antediluvian Ones made some modifications. You think my face is ugly? The rest of my body looks like a seafood buffet assembled by Dadaists.

So, could you spare a dollar? Anything helps.

True Millennial
Daniel Arthur Smith

Tyler had kept his wire-rimmed amber sunnies on when he went into the clinic. He'd taken to wearing the retro shades whether inside or out as part of his retro look—sunnies, high collar silk shirts, and a tan leather jacket. Both physically and in fashion, he was at the peak of cool. At least that was his perception. He rolled his head back against the upper pad of the reclined chair and set his gaze on the little spinning pump drawing up his blood. The pump produced a subtle, driving rhythm. It was comforting. The plasma harvested by the extraction was hidden on the other side of the big beige machine, maybe white without the sunglasses, but he didn't need to see plasma to know it was there. Seeing it didn't matter much to him anyhow. It belonged to them—at least it would as soon as he was paid. It was all about getting paid. That's why he was here; this clinic paid the best. He was fifteen minutes from seventy-five bucks, cool cash, and in twenty-five minutes, he'd be shooting pool at O'Leary's with a cheap pitcher of draft at his side.

Cheap beer, cheap buzz.

The thought sent his head lightly bouncing to the soothing rhythm of the pump—an accompaniment to a tune only he could hear.

He was in a good place.

Then she walked in.

Tyler shifted his shoulders, tilted his head to the side, and took in the show from behind his amber shades as the phlebotomist led her past to the recliner across the room.

She wasn't tall, but she wasn't short, nor was she either too thin or too full bodied—plump in the right places, she was somewhere in between. And though it was only eleven a.m., she appeared to have just stepped out of the shadows of an all-night club. Her hair was tousled in a messy, ink black, bedhead bob that fit perfectly with her dark raccoon ring mascara, black eyeliner, and all black ensemble—an oversized black biker leather, short frilly ruffle skirt, tights, and work boots.

Tyler dropped his jaw, wriggled it around, then let tip of his tongue slide side to side beneath the edge of his top front teeth as was his habit when he took an interest in something.

The woman appeared to take an interest in him too. She fixed her eyes on Tyler as she prepped for the procedure. Two strangers gazing directly upon each other in a manner anyone else would find rude.

Guided by the phlebotomist, eyes still on Tyler, she dropped her jacket behind her bare shoulders to reveal a sleeveless black cotton blouse and delicate, thin lines of script inked from below her ears, down the curve of her neck and the length of her arms to her wrists, perfectly painted to enhance her femininity. Tyler took note to try to read the script later, but for the moment, his focus was drawn to her eyes—deep and dark, drilling into him. A rush of anxiety flooded his chest, and the corner of his mouth curled up as he sensed she was about to speak, to say something, when instead she broke the spell by turning away and climbing onto her reclining chair.

The phlebotomist stepped in front of her, further separating whatever Tyler had imagined between him and the black clad woman.

He switched his focus to the large bird tattoo on the back of the phlebotomist's bald head. At least he thought it was a bird. It was one of those stencils in the native American style, like something you'd see on a Mexican pyramid, or maybe a Pacific Northwest totem. It had wings that spread ear to ear, but the body didn't really look like any animal he recognized at all. He gave up deciphering it, decided the head ink looked cool, then shifted his gaze again. First, up to the clock over the door. It was one of those cheap white discs with no real numbers, dashes for the 12, 3, 6, and 9 and dots for everything else, it didn't even have a second hand. Above the clock was a warped yellow stain in the panel of the dropped ceiling. Tyler wondered for a moment why all these clinics had the same dropped ceiling, the same wood paneling for that matter. He tilted his head forward to see what he could out the open door—the end of the reception desk was still there. A counter really. Then he looked back over toward her. The phlebotomist was still standing between them, fixing the tubes to the machine, but Tyler could see her right hand squeezing the little rubber stress toy. Her fingernails were short, the black paint thick and chipped.

He squeezed his own rubber stress toy. Ten minutes left.

A surge of yellow tinted scarlet filled the clear tube to the left of the phlebotomist and flowed up into the machine. Satisfied, the technician turned and left, leaving Tyler and the woman alone.

She had rested her phone on the frills of her short skirt and was scrolling with the thumb of her left hand.

He watched her for a minute more, but her attention never left her phone. With a sigh, he adjusted himself again and turned his head back to the clock above the door further lamenting the lack of an entertaining second hand.

"Donating?" she asked.

He spun his head back. "Excuse me?"

"Are you donating?" she asked again, her eyes still on her phone, thumb still scrolling.

"Well," his head wobbled. "For a fee."

Her eyes rolled up toward him. "This clinic pays the best," she said. "As I understand."

"You come here often?"

"First time actually."

"Really?" she asked. "This is your first time giving plasma? You seem so cool about it."

"Oh," he said with a deprecating chuckle. "Definitely not my first time. I popped that cherry in my freshman year. No. First time here. I saw a flyer on campus saying they paid seventy-five dinero. That's twenty-five more than I usually get."

"So, it pays to advertise."

Tyler nodded. "I supposed you could say that."

"You're a student then?"

"Ha, yeah."

"Why'd you laugh?"

"I've been a student for a while. Undergrad. Grad school."

"And that's funny why?"

"Oh. My parents." He shrugged and turned his head back up toward the clock. "My dad's an engineer."

"And you're not?"

"No. Not even close. Philosophy."

"I see. So, the joke's on mom and dad."

"Let's just say that days like this weren't what my parents had in mind when they sent me to school."

"I get it."

Tyler looked back over to her. "What about you?" he asked.

"What about me?" she said, letting her phone rest flat on her skirt.

"Yeah," he said. "I'm a student. How about you?"

She nodded and smiled. "Mesoamerican studies."

"You're in the graduate program?"

"Oh. I'm not a student. I'm a teacher."

"Really?"

"What do you mean really? Why do you find that surprising?"

Tyler was about to comment on her outfit or that she looked too young—but caught himself. There was no win in there. He bit softly onto the tip of his tongue, then finding himself clever, grinned, and said, "I tend to meet more students than teachers at the blood bank."

"Well," she said. "It's a shame really. More people should donate."

Relieved she wasn't offended, Tyler slowly nodded in agreement. "That they should," he said. "That they should."

Then he glanced back up at the clock.

"Hmm," she said. "You're definitely not a man of the time."

"Why'd you say that? Because I'm donating plasma?"

"No. Though that's a point too." She twirled her finger in his direction. "I was referring to the amber glasses and brown silk collar shirt. You're about forty years out of place."

"Oh. Yeah. Right."

"Those your daddy's clothes? A bit wild for an engineer."

Tyler sneered to take the burn then brought the corners of his mouth up to another grin. "My Uncle's actually."

"Really? I was just joking." She ran her eyes up and down him in a bedroom way. "Well, he certainly had a sense of style."

Tyler shrugged but before he could respond, the phlebotomist walked back into the room and directly over to Tyler's machine, interrupting the discussion between Tyler and the woman. The technician inspected the pump, tapped a couple of buttons that beeped on his touch, then began the process of unhooking Tyler.

"I'm done already?" Tyler asked.

"Yeah," said the phlebotomist. "You have good pressure."

The smirk on the phlebotomist's face creeped Tyler out, but he decided to let it slide. "Sweet," he said, then held his arms out to have the needles withdrawn and the little bandages applied.

"Alright," the phlebotomist said when he was finished. "There's cookies and juice out front. Sit for fifteen minutes then you're free to go."

Tyler pulled himself up from the chair, rolled down the sleeves of his silk shirt, and slipped on his thin tan leather jacket.

Then he flashed the woman a coy half smile. "I didn't catch your name."

"Moira," she said.

"Well, it was nice to meet you, Moira. My name's Tyler. See you next time maybe?"

"Well, Tyler. How about you wait for me, and you can see me now."

Tyler tilted his head back in faux deep thought, then gave her a full toothy grin. "Sure," he said. "I'll wait for you."

Tyler turned his attention back to the phlebotomist. "Do I need a slip or something?" he asked.

"No," said the technician. "Just stop at the desk on the way out. They'll give you your money."

"Super," said Tyler, then he turned toward the door. Before he stepped through the threshold, he spun his head back to Moira. "I'll be outside."

"Cool," said Moira.

"Cool," he echoed, then shot her yet another boyish smile.

Tyler was leaning against the wall munching on an almond cookie snagged from the clinic's snack tray when Moira walked out. She playfully twirled around to face him.

"What's the plan?" she asked, tapping the toe of one work boot against the heel of the other.

"Well," he said. "I usually take my winnings to the local dive and shoot some pool."

"Cheap beer, cheap buzz?" she asked.

"Yes," he said. "Exactly."

"I get you. But I'm not really into shooting pool. What if we get a bottle of cheap wine and take it back to my place? I live nearby and—"

"Yeah," he said, straightening up from the wall.

"Yeah?"

"Yes. A bottle of cheap wine sounds fine. After you."

A splash of warm water licked Tyler's face. The taste of salt was strong. His eyes fluttered and stung, and he made short, abrupt, feeble attempts to spit wet sand from his lips. He was on the beach, feet from the water, a gun metal steel sea beneath a deep purple horizon. The grey wet sand was warm against his cheek and jaw and waves rolled in inches from his face. Another rogue wave of white foam rushed toward him, and he thrust his weight to his shoulder to roll free from its course but, unable to move, was again washed over by the sea. Terror bombarded him as he realized he was trapped on his chest with his arms crossed beneath him, each restricting him from motion, anchoring him in a locked position.

He squeezed his eyes closed shut as another warm wave lapped his face.

Another wave immediately followed, then another, submerging him in the surf. He gasped for air, but the warm water surged, gurgled down into his lungs. Frantic and spastic, he twisted his head side to side and forced a muted scream.

Choking on the water, he clenched his eyes shut again, but this time when they opened, he found himself not on the dark beach, but on a bed beneath a puffy white blanket, in a brightly lit apartment, long floor to ceiling white curtains lightly billowing. Across the room from the foot of the bed stood Moira, naked with her back to him. A large, winged tattoo similar to—no, exactly like the one the technician at the clinic had on his scalp—was inked across her shoulder blades, from the nape of her neck, down to her perfect round ass.

A smile flashed across his face as he remembered where he was.

Images flashed through his mind of the liquor store, the dark stairwell up to her apartment, the heat of their passion, her other tattoos, on her breasts, her belly, her thighs, and then the wild roll in the hay. They'd gone on for hours. The positions, the leather straps. His brow furrowed at the image, and he looked from wrist to wrist, both lashed to the posts at the head of the bed. Yes, that had happened—she had tied him up before riding him like a bronco.

That explained the weird dream—well some of it anyway.

"Good morning," he said, finding his throat a bit dry.

"Good morning," she said without turning.

"I guess we made a night of it."

"That we did. You're quite the stallion."

"And you," he said. He looked at his wrists again and tugged, but the lashes gave no quarter. "Hey, uh…I had a great time, but would you mind untying me?"

Moira spun around, a wide smile across her face. "I kinda like you that way."

Tyler chuckled at the joke. She was a woman in her prime, her curves perfect, the delicate ink artfully painted upon her flesh enhanced her beauty, and he found himself somewhat aroused.

"So, you want to keep me as your slave?" he asked with a grin.

"Well. Yes," she said.

"I admit the thought of being your sex slave is tantalizing, but I've places I have to be. I can always come back later."

Moira approached him slowly, an exaggerated sexy swagger to her full hips. When she reached the bed, she slipped her hand beneath the foot of the blanket, and as she walked toward him, ran the tips of her fingers over his calf, then his inner thigh, stopping at his groin to fondle his member. She ran her tongue over her upper lip and sucked in a deep sigh. "Looks like something else is waking."

Tyler attempted to shift his waist, in a meager attempt to resist the excitation of her touch, only to find that his ankles were bound as well.

Again, he tugged at his bindings, to no avail.

"I uh…I think I better go."

"Shhh," she said. "Save your energy."

She gently stroked his member, and Tyler found himself unable to resist the arousal. "You're too weak to fight it," she said. "You gave that plasma yesterday and to make sure, I drugged you a little."

Tyler squinted in thought. There was the wine, but no cigarettes, no drugs. But at one point she brought out a carafe of something milky white. It had been sweet. "The shots," he said.

Moira nodded. "Yes," she said. "The shots." Then she pulled her hand from beneath the blanket and opened the drawer to her bedside table. From the drawer she pulled a paper packet and Tyler watched as she peeled it open and removed a short tube with a winged needle attached.

"Hey," he said. "What's that?"

"You know what this is," she said. "It's a butterfly needle." She set it on the side table and withdrew a bottle of rubbing alcohol from the drawer, as well as a cotton swab.

"Hey," he said. "I'm all for fun and games but I'm not into this."

Without a word, she treated the cotton with the alcohol then rubbed it onto his arm. Tyler tensed to pull away but indeed found himself weak.

"Shhh," she said again, placing the tip of the needle above his vein. "We don't want infection." Then she inserted the surgical steel.

Tyler watched as his blood filled the little hose. He found it didn't hurt. There was little sensation at all.

"The rubbing alcohol has a local anesthetic," she said, taping the small, curled hose in place. Then Moira pulled a longer coil of hose and an empty plastic blood bag from the drawer. She fixed a plastic hook to the bag, hung it to the side of the wooden drawer, then attached the other end to the connector affixed to Tyler's arm.

"What are you doing?" he asked.

"I'm going to drain you sweetie."

"Drain me?"

"Not all at once. Over time. I want to make you last."

"I...I don't understand."

"Oh honey," she said brushing the back of her hand softly against Tyler's cheek. "You see, we set up the clinic looking for something special. That's why it pays more. To lure in more donations. And Vinnie, the phlebotomist at the clinic...you remember Vinnie?"

Tyler nodded.

"Well. Vinnie called me when you came in to tell me that a rare blood type had arrived."

"My blood type is O+. It's very common."

Moira chuckled. "That's not the *type* I'm talking about. No, like I said, we were looking for something." She slid her hand down beneath the blanket over Tyler's muscular chest.

Tyler felt his nipple harden as she gently squeezed and fondled it.

"You see, sweetie, we aren't interested in A, B, or O. No. We set up the donation center to find blood with some other certain traits. Powerful, magical, genetic traits, and you—" she smiled, bent forward, and kissed his forehead. "You, my dear Tyler, have those traits. You, it turns out, are a true blood, the descendant of the great Quinametzin."

"The Kin—what?"

"The Quinametzin, they were giants among men. Literally."

"I've uh…I've never heard of them."

"Sure you have. They were children of angels, what those in Europe called the Nephilim. They once ruled the world, but they burned too brightly, their temperament was too fierce and they all but wiped themselves out, leaving only their descendants. That's you, Tyler. Your blood runs with theirs. Your blood is unique, it has very special properties. Properties that keep me young."

"What are you? Some kind of vampire or something?"

"Hardly," she said. She slid her hand down over his tight belly, down to his member, peeling the blanket away with her forearm. "But you'd be surprised how old I am. I'm a true millennial, a couple of times over. I was a priestess in the temples of your ancestors. Of course, the blood was purer then. We had to dilute it with the blood of virgins."

She pulled back the blanket, climbed up onto him, and began to grind her groin against his.

"Back then, the death was quick." Her breathing went heavy. "So much waste. But this is so much better." Moira said as she took him into her. Her back went erect, and she sighed as a quiver of excitement shot through her. "It's so much more fun to take the sacrifice this way."

ABOUT THE AUTHORS

Steven Van Patten is from Fort Greene, Brooklyn. After graduating from Long Island University on a full-tuition scholarship, he pursued a career in television production. After paying his dues, Steven went on to stage manage a plethora of TV shows, most recently *The Mel Robbins Show* and *The View*, all the while dreaming up his macabre tales.

The storyline of his first novel was born from watching horror movies as a child and noticing a lack of diversity, and character development when people of color were employed. After pouring over historical research night after night, and traveling alone to various locales, including Senegal, West Africa and Osaka, Japan, he wrote the first three installments of the **Brookwater's Curse** horror novel series, which featured a 1860s Georgia plantation slave who becomes a vampire.

After receiving much praise, several glowing reviews from various book club heavy hitters, and literary awards for each book, Steven was admitted into the Horror Writer's Association. His next two novels, '**Killer Genius: She Kills Because She Cares**' and '**Killer Genius 2: Attack of The Gym Rats**—pitted a hyper-intelligent, socially conscious female serial killer against a well-intentioned African-American detective. It debuted at NYC Comic Con in October of 2015 and was nominated for an *African-American Literary Show Award* for Best Mystery/ Suspense in 2016. Three years later, '**Hell At The Way Station**', Steven's collaboration with Marc Abbott, a horror anthology with a sort of Arabian Knights twist, won Best Anthology and Best In Sci-Free.

Visit Steven at his website: https://brookwaterscurse.com

Amy Grech has sold over 100 stories to various anthologies and magazines including: *A New York State of Fright, Apex Magazine, Beat to a Pulp: Hardboiled, Dead Harvest, Deadman's Tome Campfire Tales Book Two, Expiration Date, Fright Mare, Hell's Heart, Hell's Highway, Needle Magazine, Psycho Holiday, Real American Horror, Tales from The Lake Vol. 3, Thriller Magazine*, and many others. *New Pulp Press* published her book of noir stories, *Rage and Redemption in Alphabet City*.

She is an Active Member of the Horror Writers Association and the International Thriller Writers who lives in Brooklyn.

Visit Amy at her website: www.crimsonscreams.com

Follow Amy on Twitter: twitter.com/amy_grech

Teel James Glenn was born in Brooklyn and has traveled the world for thirty years as a Stuntman/ Fight choreographer/ Swordmaster, Jouster, Book Illustrator, Storyteller, Bodyguard and Actor (Yes he was Vega in Streetfighter: the later Years). And has done over 80 films and 55 Renaissance Faires in most of the above capacities.

He's had stories and articles printed in scores of magazines from *AfterburnSF, Classic Pulp Fiction stories, Blazing Adventures, Weird Tales*, and *Mad to Black Belt and Fantasy Tales* and a number of books published.

You can keep up with his new adventures at:

theurbanswashbuckler.com

or his blog: theurbanswashbuckler.blogspot.com

Steve Oden has worked in the publishing industry—mainly newspapers and magazines—for more than 30 years. Although retired, he provides editorial services on a consulting basis, mainly to corporate clients, and writes on assignment. His newspaper columns have appeared regularly in Tennessee and Alabama publications since 1980, winning awards from the Alabama Press Association, University of Tennessee-Tennessee Press Association, Society of Professional Journalists, National Rural Electric Cooperative Association and several wildlife conservation organizations.

Ernie Howard was born on January 29,1977 during a Minnesota blizzard. His two story telling parents almost didn't make it to the hospital in their beat up blue Cadillac. Ernie is the writer of *Write Something!,* a book about the illusion of Writers Block. *A World Without,* a Science Fiction book about the love between a husband and wife, and the darkness that can come into a marriage. *Walter,* A Science Fiction book about a boy who is an outcast who makes a friend with a man that speaks to him through his television. Ernie lives with his wife and 3 boys in Henderson, NV, where he dreams up new stories, and tries to live everyday to the fullest.

Paul B. Kohler is the International Bestselling author of the highly acclaimed novel *Linear Shift*. His recent work includes *Turn, Detour, and Reversion*, from *The Humanity's Edge Trilogy*, along with several short stories. His short story, *Rememorations*, was included in *The Immortality Chronicles* - The Best Anthology of the Year as voted in the 2016 Predators and Editors Readers Poll. *Rememorations* was also nominated for Best American Science Fiction.

Visit Paul's main site paulkohler.net for news and updates

Charles Barouch's quest to never stop learning has made him a fiction author, a journalist, a teacher, and a technologist. You can find some of his other fiction writings on Amazon, Nook, and Kobo. His current journalism is in the pages of International Spectrum. You can hear him speak at Otakon and Spectrum Conferences.

And, he's been known to hang out on social media platforms if you'd like to talk.

Hunter C. Eden is a Denver-based essayist and dark fantasy writer whose work has appeared in **Weird Tales**, **City Slab**, and **Ravenous Monster Horror Webzine**.

Jessica West (a.k.a. West1Jess) is currently pursuing a state of self-induced psychosis, also known as writing. In the past, she has worked for Wal-Mart, a lawyer, and a bank. Now if she could just get a couple years experience with the IRS and the NSA, world domination is in the bag.

Jess lives in Acadiana with three daughters still young enough to think she's cool and a husband who knows better but likes her anyway.

For news and updates visit west1jess.com

Daniel Arthur Smith is a USA Today bestselling author. His titles include *Spectral Shift*, *Hugh Howey Lives, The Cathari Treasure, The Somali Deception*, and a few other novels and short stories. He also curates the phenomenal short fiction series *Tales from the Canyons of the Damned* and *Frontiers of Speculative Fiction*.

He was raised in Michigan and graduated from Western Michigan University where he studied philosophy, with focus on cognitive science, meta-physics, and comparative religion. He began his career as a bartender, barista, poetry house proprietor, teacher, and then became a technologist and futurist for the Fortune 100 across the Americas and Europe.

Daniel has traveled to over 300 cities in 22 countries, residing in Los Angeles, Kalamazoo, Prague, Crete, and now writes in Manhattan where he lives with his wife and young sons.

For news and updates visit danielarthursmith.com

www.ingramcontent.com/pod-product-compliance
Lightning Source LLC
Chambersburg PA
CBHW030342180626
46812CB00007B/2731